LADIES O

The Lady's Battle

ANNE R BAILEY

INKBLOT PRESS

Ebook ISBN: 978-1-990156-42-7

Print Book ISBN: 978-1-990156-43-4

Please note this book is written in US English (example: colour is correctly spelled color).

For all my readers.
Without you none of this would've been possible.

The Widowed Bride

Choosing Him

Other

The Stars Above

You can also follow the author at: www.inkblotpressco.ca

CHAPTER 1

1259, GASCONY

The two knights thundered towards each other, their polished armor flashing silver in the sunlight. They lowered their lances and time stopped; Eleanor held her breath.

As they met, the sounds of splintering wood and a horse's alarmed whinny filled the air. One horse reared. The knight on its back slid from the saddle and fell to the ground with a thud. The crowd roared its approval.

But Eleanor's heart hammered in her chest as her gaze fixed itself upon the fallen knight. He did not move. Would this be the first casualty of the day?

Jousting was a dangerous business. Accidents happened all too frequently, even though the aim was merely for men to show off their prowess, not to kill each other. Amidst the panic, the other knight, dropped his lance and reached over the divide to grab the panicked horse's reins. He guided both horses out of the way of the fallen man. Now there would be no danger of him being crushed by a stray hoof.

Eleanor stood with the rest of the watching crowd to applaud as the victor turned to face them. But rather than ride towards the raised pavilion, where she waited to award the prize, he rode back to his opponent and slide from his horse — a challenge for anyone in such heavy armor. The crowd murmured as he removed his helmet and kneeled by the fallen man's side.

When the victorious knight helped his opponent to his feet, cheers rang around the tiltyard at such a show of chivalry and humbleness.

At last, he turned towards her. Her heart raced at his broad smile and shining blue eyes.

Her husband, Edward, Prince of England, came forward and bowed to her. He'd faced all challengers and won. A thrill coursed through her at the knowledge he was hers and she was his.

As she crowned him with a coronet of braided ivy, her eyes never left his. All she wanted was to slink away with him and spend the day in his arms. From the heat in his eyes, she could tell his thoughts weren't far from her own.

But, alas, it could not be so. Before they could think of their desires, they had to think of their duty. Edward turned to the crowd and waved, which only intensified their cheering.

As he walked off the tournament field, followed by his eager squires, she noted how he favored his left leg. He'd been hurt. Her throat clenched with that familiar worry for her husband.

Forcing her attention back to the crowd and the other

knights, she went through the motions of handing out the rest of the prizes, and then invited the jugglers and acrobats onto the field to entertain the spectators.

By the time she retired within the castle walls, the sun was high overhead and the heat had become unbearable.

Glad to be inside, Eleanor ordered the servants to prepare a bath for her husband and selected fresh clothes for him. As she was inspecting his bedchamber, his steward, Robert Leyburn, came in and bowed low. He looked anxious, and she motioned him over.

"I didn't mean to interrupt you, My Lady," he said, his eyes downcast.

"Nonsense," she said, waiting patiently for him to go on. Robert was the third son of a landed knight, but the family had never been wealthy. By a stroke of luck, he entered Edward's service and rose in the ranks. While he was utterly loyal, Robert could be timid, filled with uncertainty that he didn't belong here. Now he shifted his weight from one foot to another as he considered how to begin.

"A letter has arrived from William de Valence for Lord Edward," he said, then stopped, unsure of how to go on. "The messenger gave me the gist of the contents. He insisted I hear him and bring the letter to Prince Edward directly. This was even after I had insisted that the Prince would not receive him if his parents had sent them from England in disgrace."

She watched him, understanding the apprehension gnawing at him. He felt unsteady in these trying times. With so much unrest in England, the factions at court were vying for power — yet another thing he had no taste for.

"Then it must be a matter of some urgency," Eleanor said, hoping the comment would prompt him.

"The Lusignans wish to come here. He reminds his nephew — half-nephew — of their familial bonds." Robert Leyburn sniffed. He was sensitive to proper rank and distinction.

Eleanor let this sink in. Already her imagination had taken flight, picturing how her father-in-law would take the news. When he had told Edward to leave England weeks ago, their relationship had been tense. Now, if Edward allowed his exiled relations to visit, it would look like Edward was setting up a faction against his father. Queen Alienor, paranoid as she was, would be quick to use this against him.

"Perhaps the request is innocent enough," Eleanor said at last, mulling over whether this could be a trap to draw Edward into danger. "We shall have to see this letter." Then, remembering to defer to her husband, she said, "My husband will know how to respond." She held out her hand for it.

After the briefest hesitation, Robert Leyburn relinquished it.

"I would never seek to meddle, but I feel compelled to warn you that the Queen will not be pleased if he agrees to meet with him—"

He was cut off by the arrival of Edward himself.

"Nothing would please my mother more than if I would've remained a child clutching at her skirts," Edward said, a twinge of disrespect in his voice. "But I am a grown man now and I will make my own decisions. Let me see this letter."

Eleanor handed it to him, wishing she'd had the chance to read it and form an opinion first.

He scanned it quickly and then folded it up. "I shall write my reply in due course. Thank you, Sir Robert, for your continued care of me. I know you do it out of love." He clapped his steward on the shoulder, dismissing him.

Eleanor waved off the other servants and set about helping Edward undress.

"It's been a long day, Eleanor," he said. As she stared at his face she saw no tiredness in his eyes, only mischief.

"You smell of horse and sweat," she said, wrinkling her nose in disgust.

"But I won the day, did I not? Should I not be rewarded with your love?" He trailed his fingertips down her arms.

"I will praise your prowess and valor endlessly. You know my heart is yours but, you shall have nothing more until you have a bath."

There was a playful smile upon his lips as he released her and slipped into the scalding water with a sigh.

Eleanor took a vial of rose oil from the locked cupboard and let a few drops fall into the water. As she scrubbed his back with a rough towel, she said, "If I were to guess, I would say you've made up your mind to meet with your uncles." Edward was usually a rational man, but lately his parents had been driving him to make impulsive decisions.

"There's no reason why I cannot meet with him and hear what he has to say. We both know the banishment was my mother's doing. She's always been jealous of the honors and love my father heaps on them. She covets anything that is given to others."

"Then you better watch out, because Gascony might be next on her list."

He scoffed. "She rues the day my father invested me with lands of my own. At the time she thought I would be a placid vassal at her command, but she quickly realized I would not bend to her every whim and desire. Especially when it goes against our people's best interest."

Eleanor put a hand on his bare arm in an effort to stop his treasonous words. Then she went over to the bed to examine the tunic laid out for him. She'd embroidered the deep blue silk herself. Beneath her fingertips she could feel the raised embroidery of the silver foliage interspersed with fleur-de-lys.

She could hear Edward muttering to himself as he scrubbed the remaining dirt and dust from his skin.

Her husband was chafing under the yoke of his parents. He wanted independence but was constantly held back.

When he'd been made Duke of Gascony, Edward thought his chance had come at last. Instead, he discovered he was shackled to a troublesome province, beholden to his parents' goodwill. Despite its wealth, the lords of Gascony were always causing trouble and Edward struggled to keep the peace. In England, they blamed him when trade fell and accused him of being an ineffectual commander when a lord rebelled. Eleanor knew Edward could prevail if the King did not insist on keeping him short of funds. It was a miracle that Edward had held on to Gascony at all.

It was growing apparent that the King and Queen did not trust Edward with an army of his own. How could his parents think he would betray them? Was he not already heir to the crown of England? What nightmares haunted their waking hours?

Though still childless herself, Eleanor couldn't understand how Alienor distrusted her son. Where was her love and pride in him? Didn't she realize she was creating an enemy of Edward the more she tried to meddle in his affairs?

"Do you think Robert Leyburn is to be trusted?" she asked, smoothing out the sleeve on the bed.

"He is my man through and through. His only fault is his abundance of caution. There is nothing my parents can accuse me of if I meet with the Lusignans. They were exiled from England. But this is Gascony and I was never prohibited from seeing them."

Eleanor looked over her shoulder, smiling ruefully at him. "I do believe that was implied when your mother had them sent from the kingdom. To show them friendship is to set yourself up against your mother."

Edward motioned for her to bring him a robe. He got out of the bath and settled on a chair by the fire.

"I must go to ensure that everything is in place for the banquet," Eleanor said, giving him a kiss on his forehead. "We shall prevail."

"Come what may." He gave her hand a squeeze.

Down below in the great hall, servants were carrying in trestle tables and covering them with linen cloths. On the high dais, banners hung on the freshly frescoed walls. The canopy of estate encompassed their two high-backed chairs of solid walnut intricately carved with hunting motifs and the coat of arms of both England and Castile. Among the coat of arms stitched delicately into the cloth her eyes always caught on the familiar gold with the three bands of azure representing Ponthieu, the French county which she would inherit from her mother. It gave her a sense of pride to see it, even though Edward's far grander emblems as Prince of England, and Duke of Gascony eclipsed it.

Stepping back, she took in the room again. From a quick glance, it would be clear to all that here sat a great lord and his lady. None could doubt Edward's power and importance.

For this banquet she'd ordered garlands of flowers to decorate the tables and for the servants to hang up tapestries depicting the brave deeds of knights. The largest of these was one of Saint George slaying the dragon. Eleanor nodded her approval at the arrangement before informing a servant to remind the steward to serve the Burgundian wine.

It was then that Peter of Savoy swaggered into the hall, a hand on his hip as though this was all his. He spotted her and smiled before dipping into a bow, as was customary. He was Queen Alienor's uncle, and at the moment her most trusted advisor and favorite. Rather than send the funds Edward had requested to hire mercenaries, his parents had sent Peter to assist with the management of Gascony. His advice was unwelcome and often unhelpful. Both Eleanor and her husband were certain he was here as a spy. He certainly tried to throw his weight around, and acted as though Gascony was his to rule.

"And where is Lord Edward?" he asked, rubbing his nose. "I have heard the Lusignans are on their way to court him."

Eleanor blinked, stunned by his knowledge and the fact he would openly discuss it.

"He will be down shortly, but I don't see how this is any business of yours, Lord Peter," she said, in her haughtiest tone.

He grinned, his head tilting to the side as though he were a lion amused by the mewling of a mere barn cat. "It is in my interest to protect the Prince against the influence of others who would sway him down a path of..." He paused, searching for the right word, but then threw off his attempts at metaphor. "It would not serve him to set himself up against his parents."

"He is a dutiful son and always has been. The Lusignans are kin; he owes them a modicum of respect. As far as we are concerned, they have done nothing to warrant us refusing to see them." She waited for him to argue but he was at a loss for words.

Indeed, the only thing the Lusignans could be accused of was becoming overmighty subjects. It wasn't their fault the Queen felt threatened by their power and wealth.

Lord Peter shook his head. "I see the pair of you are determined to be stubborn children rather than have the sense to follow the example of your betters."

Eleanor arched an imperious brow.

"Uncle, I was looking everywhere for you." Prince Edward's voice echoed around the vast hall. As he approached them, his gaze flicked to Eleanor's. He took her hand and brought it to his lips. "My Lady, I hope all is well? Anyone who causes you distress should be thrown into a dungeon."

In the deafening silence that followed, Lord Peter kept twisting the ring on his finger.

"M-my—"

Eleanor interrupted his indignant stuttering. "All is well. I was merely informing Lord Peter that you look forward to hosting your uncles. It has been a long time since you have seen them, and we shall certainly have much to discuss with them."

Lord Peter bowed his head, though judging by the clenched fists at his sides, he was struggling to hold himself back.

"Perhaps you'd like to help me organize another tournament in their honor, Uncle?"

"I'd be happy to," Lord Peter said through gritted teeth.

"Excellent. My mother always assures me how helpful and eager to please you are."

Sensing her husband was pushing this proud man too far, Eleanor put a hand on Edward's forearm and said, "Shall I show you the plans I made for the library?"

"Of course. Lord Peter, we shall speak later in private about the upcoming visit."

"My Lord," he said, with a curt bow.

As Eleanor's eyes followed his retreating form, she could feel his seething indignation.

"You must tread carefully with him, my love," she said to Edward.

"He needs to be put in his place," he replied, looking at her as if her words were a betrayal.

"You are fresh from the tournament, and your judgement is clouded. He can become a thorn in our side if he wishes. So try to be calm and think diplomatically."

"Diplomacy is your area of expertise." He gave her hand a squeeze. "But I shall keep my mouth shut around him if you wish. He acts like he can order me around; it drives me to madness."

"Let me distract you with something else then," she said, as they reached the table where the architect had laid out the plans for the renovations to the old chapel. "It would be a shame to let the old chapel sit unused. I thought perhaps repurposing it as a place of study would be a suitable alternative."

"And the cost of such a venture?" he asked, eyeing the plans.

"As you can see, there wouldn't be much to do. Some shelves, and tables brought in. A fresh coat of paint on the walls too. The only major work would be to fix the roof." She could tell he was unsure. Maybe he was thinking about how he'd make use of the space himself. "It wouldn't suit as an armory."

"Can you read my mind?" His eyes were full of mirth as he regarded her.

"There's far too much light. It would rust the metal and it's too far from the blacksmith," she said.

He laughed. "A little sunlight wouldn't rust a sword. But anyway, I can see how determined you are. Go ahead, build your library. Heavens knows you need a place for all your books. Don't think I haven't noticed the collection in your solar."

She pushed lightly against his arm for teasing her. "You appreciate all my learning when it is time to entertain foreign ambassadors and negotiate with Italian merchants."

"I would do well to remember that." He placed a kiss on her brow.

The banquet began with a short ceremony honoring the day's victors. Men were praised for their prowess and applauded for their feats of bravery. Wine was poured freely into eager cups. It wouldn't be long before they were all drunk.

Eleanor sat beside her husband under the cloth of estate. He was busy recounting the day's events with his friends. Tales of their exploits grew with each telling. She remained withdrawn, focused on ensuring her ladies-in-waiting behaved themselves rather than on celebrating with her husband.

A part of her wondered if he was being too hasty in accepting a visit from his half-uncles. In the end, it might be more trouble than it was worth. Gascony was his, but he held on to it by the skin of his teeth.

As young as Edward was, he was already a veteran of the battlefield. The Gascon lords constantly challenged his rule, and then there was the Count of Toulouse who thought Gascony ought to belong to him. He was always riding out with a small force to protect his lands. The situation was complicated. Made even more so by the unfulfilled promises of more troops and funds from his parents. When troops did arrive, they were a quarter of the number asked for. As for funds? That was laughable. Knowing all this, how should they proceed?

Eleanor's head began to ache.

"My Lady," her husband whispered to her, and she blinked. "You are distracted."

"I am," she admitted.

"Shall we dance? Perhaps that will make you forget your troubles."

It took Eleanor a moment to collect herself. She had been so distracted she had not heard the minstrels take up their positions. With a nod, she let Edward lead her to the center of the room, where the other dancers waited.

She moved with all the grace and poise a princess ought to possess, but her heart was not in it even as she glided towards her husband. As she spun, Eleanor felt the hairs on the nape of her neck stand on end. When she craned her neck she spotted Peter of Savoy watching them. His expression was cold.

CHAPTER 2

1259, GASCONY

Edward rode out with a large party of attendants and armed guards to meet the Lusignans on the road and escort them back to the castle.

A part of Eleanor wished she had gone with them. Words would be exchanged without her knowledge and she worried her husband would make promises he couldn't keep.

However, Edward had all but forbidden her to go with him.

Not too long ago a party of their trusted servants had been ambushed on the road. One man had died in the resulting skirmish. With the roads so unpredictable, he had preferred her to stay behind and oversee preparations for the arrival of these honored guests. Besides, if she hadn't stayed behind the task would have fallen to Peter of Savoy and who knows what mischief he would've caused.

Over the last few weeks, Eleanor, aware of his increasing dislike of her, had him watched. She didn't trust him.

Despite what he believed to be her frivolous nature, she had paid her staff handsomely to keep a close eye on the comings and goings of all their visitors. Locked away in her office at this very moment was a letter to Queen Alienor written by Peter. She'd painstakingly removed the seal without breaking it. Once she had finished studying it for any secret code or message, she would reseal it and send it on its way.

As far as she could see he was simply reassuring Alienor that while Edward was meeting with the Lusignans, he meant no harm by it.

The letter had rankled Eleanor in its underestimation of Edward. His parents and even his maternal uncle saw him as a weakling. One who was dangerous only because he was old enough to carry a sword. They believed him stupid enough to plot to usurp the throne. What an imagination they had. It irritated her no end that this family could not simply get along. It would be far easier to work together than go on forever distrusting each other.

The biggest impediments to Edward's success were, ironically, his own parents.

It made her think of her own loving family. Even after the death of her father, they had lived together harmoniously. After he ascended the throne, her brother continued to nurture relationships with all his siblings. He could see the value in each of them and he contrived to make the most of their strengths. It had made Castile strong.

In England, the royal family was always at each other's throats.

And yet, here she was spying. Was she any better?

Eleanor wasn't naïve. Her enemies and friends alike were intercepting her correspondences, trying to gain some insight into her inner thoughts. She had to put aside her scruples in order to survive. It was the way of the world. She'd learned at the feet of her sainted father the intricacies of how a kingdom was run.

Knowledge was more valuable than gold, so she let the coins slip through her fingers in exchange for manuscripts, books, and secrets.

She watched a team of servants hang colorful banners displaying Edward's heraldry interspersed with ribbons over the gateway. Troubadours were waiting on the parapets to serenade their guests with beautiful music, and she would be ready with the ladies of the household to greet her husband's kin. It gave the castle a festive air.

In the world of politics, appearance was everything. Something as small as excellent housekeeping could make all the difference in a negotiation.

"Put your friends and enemies alike at ease," her father had said.

Indeed, over the last few years, she'd found this to be true. A pleasant visit often smoothed the way to friendship or at the very least a peaceful accord. Many times it simply took an extravagant meal to win an alliance. No one could think of fighting when their bellies were full.

Eleanor only wished their finances weren't in such an abysmal state. No one knew how heavily they borrowed from lenders, but they'd be in a worse position if they didn't keep their vassals and friends happy. It was the price they had to pay.

A gaggle of maids emerged from the castle with brooms and swept the cobblestones in the courtyard in front of the keep. Later, they would strew dried rose petals on the ground so the air would be fragrant and sweet.

Among the visitors, there was one person Eleanor was particularly interested in impressing.

Traveling with her Lusignan husband was Joan de Munschensi, the great English heiress. She'd been forced to flee England and recently reunited with her family in France. Eleanor could only imagine the hardships she had faced in the past year. The Oxford Parliament had deprived her first of her home and then her inheritance for no other reason than who she'd married. In a just world, this could not have occurred. The silver lining in all of this was that now Eleanor might have a companion to spend her days with.

Above on the parapets, men unfurled flags and at last everything was in place. A sense of contentment filled Eleanor.

She spared a moment to ensure she looked her best. For this occasion she'd chosen an emerald green gown cut in the English fashion, with a girdle studded with precious pearls about her waist.

The chamberlain and steward of the household had arrived, and the party was ready to greet their travelers. She noted drily that Peter of Savoy had waited until the last moment to arrive. A sign of disrespect Eleanor struggled to ignore.

It wasn't long before they heard the distant sounds of the retinue approaching. Heralds blared their trumpets while drums beat out a happy marching tune.

At a signal from a guard on the parapet the troubadours began to play. When her husband and his uncles rode through the gatehouse they were greeted by the pleasant music and scent of a summertime palace.

Edward was beaming in the saddle with no sign of any uncertainty in his features. Eleanor was overcome with appreciation for how handsome and powerful he looked. Indeed, he was like a knight straight out of an Arthurian ballad.

Stepping forward, she held out her arms in greeting, and he characteristically left all decorum behind to sweep her off her feet and twirl her around.

"My Lord," she said, mortified and thrilled all at once.

Setting her back on her feet, he bowed to her and she curtseyed to him, then allowed him to take her hand to draw her to his waiting uncles.

Guy de Lusignan was a tall, broad-chested man, a warrior through and through, but his eyes sparked with amusement as he took in the pair of them.

"I see now why my nephew is content to spend his days in the seclusion of Gascony," he said, then bowing low greeted her formally. "It is an honor to meet you, Princess."

"You as well, My Lord Uncle," Eleanor said, her gaze sweeping past him and the others to settle on the grand lady in the party. Joan de Munchensi was a beautiful woman, only a few years older than Eleanor. She was impeccably dressed in a blue gown etched with fleur-de-lys, and a white, fur-lined mantle.

In this world of men she inhabited, Eleanor couldn't help harboring the secret hope that in Joan she might find an equal and a friend.

Next to come forward was the Bishop of Winchester, Aymer de Valence. Although exiled from his diocese, he still wore the robes of his position and had a haughty expression she didn't care for. But William Lusignan, the youngest of the three, was nearly as handsome as her own husband and was clearly keen on observing the social niceties.

The way his gaze kept drifting to Joan told Eleanor he cherished his wife dearly. A man who loved his wife was a good man in her books, and she greeted him warmly.

"May I introduce you to my wife, Lady Joan," William said, motioning her forward.

"It's a pleasure to meet you at last," Eleanor said, bowing her head politely. "Though I wish the circumstances were more favorable for everyone."

Joan's serene expression shifted to one of mirth. "Indeed, but now we are at last in each other's company I am keen to get to know you better."

It appeared they were of one mind. Eleanor turned to her husband for permission to go on. He inclined his head, and she turned back to the gathered crowd in the courtyard.

"You have traveled far, my lords," she said, loud enough that all could hear. "I hope the little banquet I have planned will go a long way to soothing away your weariness. Welcome to Gascony."

Applause followed her announcement, together with enthusiasm for the hospitality that awaited them. Conscious of the state they would arrive in, Eleanor had arranged for maids to line up along the pathway to the keep holding basins of fresh water and linen so they might wash their hands and take this cloaks before entering.

The great hall had been cleaned and prepared meticulously for their arrival. The candles in the chandelier were lit, and sconces on the walls blazed with light from oil lamps.

The tables from the highest to the lowest were laden with enough breads and dried fruits to sate the appetite of the hungriest traveler. As her husband finished receiving his guests, servants brought up roasted meats from the kitchens below. Wine was poured generously, and soon many people were rosy cheeked and eager to make merry.

Not wanting the party to degenerate into a drunken mess, Eleanor motioned to the steward with a crook of her finger, and ordered him to water down the wine.

At Eleanor's insistence, Joan sat on her left, and she turned her attention to getting to know her guest.

"Have you been enjoying your time in France?"

"As much as one could, given the circumstances," Joan said, dabbing at the corner of her mouth with a napkin. "I wish we had come of our own volition."

Eleanor nodded, surprised but pleased that she was so forthright in her opinions. She certainly didn't come across as one of those delicate ladies who were ignorant of the goings on of the world.

She glanced at Joan more carefully, noting faint, dark circles under her eyes and the tension in her features. Eleanor felt a wave of pity.

Queen Alienor and Eleanor had never seen eye to eye,

so her animosity had come as no surprise. But Joan had been her ward and been raised by Alienor since she was a young child. How could the Queen have been so cruel to her? It had been the King who arranged her marriage to William, his younger half-brother. Perhaps the Queen had not approved.

Yet, it did not make sense to punish Joan.

Eleanor could only guess at the tumult of emotions coursing through her. Alienor's friendship was always fickle. Even her brother, Peter of Savoy, had been sent away against his will to watch over Gascony for her. Eleanor was sure he was keen to be back in England where the riches were far greater and life was more comfortable.

"For all the upheaval of the last few months, I am grateful to be reunited with my husband. He is a kind, honorable man. He didn't deserve to be cast out of the country because the King favored him," Joan said, with a shake of her head.

"He certainly did not," Eleanor said, though she was mindful to tread carefully. She wouldn't be stupid enough to lower her guard and say anything that could be used against her. "It wasn't the King's wish to remove his half-brothers. Even here in Gascony we heard how Simon de Montfort harassed Parliament."

"He is our greatest enemy," Joan all but whispered. "I hate how righteous he pretends to be but who is dining on my gold plate? Who is profiting off my lands?"

Eleanor gave a shake of her head. "Justice will be done."

"I pray to God it will." Joan glanced around the hall, her expression falling back into one of demureness. "I just don't know how long we can go on like this. Jumping from house to house, little more than beggars."

A fresh pang of injustice sparked a rage Eleanor struggled to contain. "Rest assured neither Prince Edward nor I see you as such. We wish we could provide you with more assistance, but in the meantime we welcome you into our household with open arms. I know my husband is eager to have his kin with him. We have also been sent far from home."

Joan leaned in to whisper, "Yet, I see Peter of Savoy is dining with us."

Eleanor grimaced and amended her words. "Rest assured he has been placed here at the behest of the Queen. As you can see, Edward is not trusted even by his own mother."

Joan let out a soft laugh. "Then what hope can I have of a reconciliation?" She gave her a sidelong look, as if she had not meant to say the words and was wondering what Eleanor's reaction would be.

"The King will be reasonable. I am sure he will find a way to restore his half-brothers."

"Do you think Prince Edward will speak on our behalf?"

Eleanor was startled by the bluntness of the question. Had this been the reason the Lusignans came all the way to Gascony? She'd known it wasn't out of some special love or consideration, yet the pang of hurt and disappointment was still there. Nothing in life came freely. Even love.

Joan waited for her reply, her eyes never leaving her face, but Eleanor took her time answering.

"Edward loves his family. He owes his obedience to his

parents. If he were to speak out on your behalf, it would cause a rift in the family. It is bad enough we allowed you to come visit us. Or so we've been told," she said, inclining her head toward Lord Peter. She reached across the table for the pitcher of wine, filled her glass and then sipped. It tasted bitter on her tongue.

"Please," said Joan, "rest assured we are also eager to support you and Edward in your travails with the Queen. She is clearly not one to be trusted. She will set the kingdom afire before she gives in."

Eleanor regarded Joan's pale features. She looked unwell. Eleanor was once again reminded of the hardship she had encountered in the past few months. Deciding to be charitable, she motioned for her lady's maid to come forth.

"Is everything ready in Lady Joan's room?"

"It is, milady."

"Excellent," she said, then turned to Joan. "Why don't we retire? I am sure you could use a bath and somewhere quiet to rest. We can talk more candidly in your rooms where we won't be overheard."

Joan hesitated for the briefest moment. Her gaze flicked to her husband, as though asking for permission. When he nodded, she smiled up at Eleanor.

"I think that would be excellent."

Eleanor stood, which caused quite a stir in the great hall as all fell silent to watch her.

"We ladies shall retire for the night," she announced. "You gentlemen may go on playing but we have matters of state to attend to."

There was laughter among the men.

Eleanor bit back a secret smile of her own. As she

escorted Joan through the palace, she stopped to show her a gallery and point out a few choice spots for a reprieve if the heat of the castle grew too great.

"You are quite frank in your speech," Lady Joan said.

It took Eleanor a moment to realize what she was referring to. "Ah, yes. I think it amuses them when I make such outlandish claims. If I say nothing, then they wonder what I get up to at all hours of the day. But I find that if I just tell them, they never take me seriously." She stopped as they rounded a corner. "Though they should."

"You are not what I expected," Lady Joan said.

Eleanor arched her brows.

Flushing pink, Lady Joan looked away. "I meant that as a compliment, Princess. In England, the Queen is keen to spread terrible rumors about you. I am afraid even though I know of her duplicitous nature, they still colored my opinion of you."

Eleanor shrugged. "That is the way it is. She liked me well enough when I first came to England. I am sure Queen Alienor expected a biddable girl she could mold, not an outspoken, educated scholar. But if she is disappointed then she ought to complain to the ambassadors who negotiated this marriage. It is no fault of mine that we don't get along. On the other hand, I am grateful for my husband. He is a treasure."

"He is quite devoted to you. The moment he met us on the road he mentioned how he wished for us to be introduced."

It pleased Eleanor to know she was at the forefront of her husband's mind.

"So now tell me, how were things at the English court

when you left? Is Simon de Montfort still reigning supreme?"

Eleanor pushed open the double doors to their guest chambers. Inside, plush carpets had been laid out on the floor. A large fire blazed in the grate while a tub filled with steaming water awaited Joan.

"This is quite luxurious."

"Traveling on the road is not pleasant. I know this from personal experience. France has its share of troubles, but we have some luxuries here that I often take advantage of." Eleanor motioned for the waiting maids to come forth with trays filled with soaps and perfumes and glass vials containing precious scented oils for the hair and skin. "You must allow my women to pamper you. I shall wait for you in the adjoining room then we can talk."

"I appreciate this more than words can express."

Eleanor's smile was strained as she left the room. Indeed, she hoped that Joan would be more amenable to her. She needed her to be honest.

As she waited, Eleanor moved around the presence chamber examining the embroidered cushions and the tray of sweetmeats. After an hour Joan emerged, looking far more relaxed. Dressed in a loose gown with her hair in a braid, she made her way to an empty chair. It was then that Eleanor took in the slight swell of her belly. Was she with child?

"Is there something else you require?" Eleanor asked, her mind in a whirl. This could be a real bargaining chip. With an heir on the way, both Joan and William would be eager to return to England as soon as possible, and have their lands restored, too.

"You have been generous in your hospitality. I want for nothing."

Eleanor took a seat across from her. "Nothing?" she asked lightly. "Not even your titles back?"

Joan laughed. "If you have them tucked away somewhere I would appreciate them."

"While you are with us, I hope we shall have ample opportunity to ride about the countryside. There is a beautiful deer park nearby and I would love for you to see it. The weather is finer here than across the channel so take advantage of it while you can." Eleanor smoothed her skirts. "As you can see, I am quite determined for us to be friends. But now I am talking far too much. Tell me about yourself."

Joan leaned back in her chair, her shoulders slumping. "There's not much to tell, I'm afraid. Everything I valued was snatched away from me. But at odd times I do enjoy embroidering and I adore music."

"Then I shall make sure you shall have plenty of opportunities to do both. Our husbands shall busy themselves hunting and playing cards well into the night. We shall have to learn to be content without them."

Joan looked shocked once again.

"Have I upset you again? My brashness will be my doom."

With a shake of her head Joan laughed. "No. Nonsense. I was merely caught off guard. William says I am far too silent. I have my upbringing to blame for that. The Queen expected a certain decorum from her ladies. I was never encouraged to be outspoken."

Eleanor nodded sympathetically. At court only Queen Alienor could command attention. She feared anyone eclipsing her and was eager others should be mere shadows waiting on her hand and foot. If she stopped to consider the Queen's situation, Eleanor could sympathize. Hated by the common people and resented by the nobles, her position was tenable at best.

Could Eleanor do any better? Would she?

Whenever thoughts of the future entered her mind she felt uncertain. Yet, her good humor prevailed. At the very least she was far more open handed, so no one could complain she was miserly.

"The two of you seem so happy together," said Eleanor.

"He loves me dearly."

"You sound as though that surprises you."

Joan laughed. "Oh, I wouldn't have been his first choice of bride. I am well aware of how I was foisted upon him."

"A pretty, wealthy bride with intelligence to boot? How could you even say that?"

From the way Joan had begun to play with the ties of her robe, Eleanor began to suspect there was much she didn't know. Gossip took a while to reach Gascony. Perhaps William had his heart set on another bride.

"Well, it all worked out in the end. Despite this latest upset."

"Yes, it has," Joan said, her serious expression breaking at last. "How are things here? We know that Gascony is a troubled region and you are kept short of money."

"And men," Joan admitted, but added quickly, "though we are safe enough within these walls. It would behoove the King to shore up his borders and provide his nobles with the funds and men to defend them. There should be no reason why the French lords feel they can raid our borders or test our defenses."

"They say you are sympathetic to the French."

The words slipped out of Joan's lips unbidden.

"I am surprised," Eleanor said, her mouth dry. "Why?"

"Your mother, and the fact that you will one day govern Ponthieu."

"I am married. My lands are just as much Edward's," Eleanor sniffed, indignant at the unfairness.

Joan chuckled. "Yes. I understand how you feel. When everything goes well our husbands get the credit as lords of our land. But when things go sour it must be our doing. Somehow."

"I've always felt inheritance laws in England are unfair in many regards. I hope to rectify it one day."

"That would be something marvelous to see."

"And about as likely to happen as me performing a miracle." Eleanor put a hand to her lips. "Now I shall have to confess this sin." She gave a shake of her head. "I speak without thinking and it gets me into trouble all the time. Now tell me, what is your husband hoping to get from us? He must know the King does not listen to his son."

"We know you have little influence," Joan said, shaking out her gown so it billowed about her feet. "But Prince Edward is still the heir. People look to him as the future leader of our nation." She must have seen Eleanor's withdrawn expression because she hurried to say, "It is not treasonous to say so. Merely fact, should God will it."

"Amen," Eleanor whispered. Then clearing her throat she said, "He is also an obedient son. He would never set himself up against his father. Nor do we have the funds or resources for such an endeavor, should we wish to act."

Joan nodded again. "We know. Which is precisely why the King and Queen keep you in a state of near poverty. But whether or not you will it, disenfranchised people are turning to you and your husband."

"We would never plot treason." Eleanor said this with such fervor that she surprised herself.

"Simon de Montfort has the support of the majority of the barons, but even they know Simon cannot rule. He has no claim to the English throne."

"I am sure one could be fabricated," said Eleanor. "I am not so well versed in the genealogy of the English noble lords as I am of the Castilian, but there might be some royal sister or uncle of a long-ago king he could claim to be descended from."

"If he did, he would lose all the support he has gained. They would see him as a power-hungry man who over-reaches himself."

Eleanor motioned for her lady-in-waiting to bring her a glass of wine with the flick of her wrist and a patient smile.

"Is that not exactly what he is? Whether he makes any claims on the throne or not."

Joan gave her a dry smile and inclined her head. "But you must agree that he makes a compelling argument about why we should curb the current King's power."

"He is a dangerous man." Eleanor could not commit to more. She dared not. Besides, there was something she hated about him. He certainly knew how to charm a crowd and exactly what to say. There were problems with the way the realm was being governed, but she didn't see how his solutions would fix matters. If anything, they would line the pockets of his friends and supporters rather than the Queen's.

"There are others you might not have considered who'd be willing to help," Joan said.

"Who do you mean?"

"The French King."

Eleanor felt her throat clench. This was not the way she had envisioned this conversation going.

CHAPTER 3

1259, GASCONY

Edward was running his hands through her hair, but it didn't soothe the growing headache.

"I think she is with child," Eleanor said, unable to bring herself to say more.

"I was not told. I am surprised a woman in her condition traveled all this way."

Eleanor propped herself up on her elbows and regarded her husband. "I don't think she had much of a choice. And what do you think? The moment a woman is pregnant she must be confined to her rooms? You should've told me about this before we were married."

"And what would you have done?" He reached out and tapped her nose.

"Run the other way," she said, swatting his hand away, though a playful grin spread across her features. "At the very least I would've claimed sanctuary in a convent."

"I can't imagine you as a nun," he said, his fingers returning to their ministrations.

Despite the twinge of desire his touch evoked, her mind was focused on graver matters.

"Has William or Guy spoken to you yet?"

"About?"

"Edward, this is serious. Look at me."

"I am."

"Have they?"

At last she could see he was taking her seriously. He gave a nod. "They are sympathetic. Governing Gascony is not the honor I thought it was. I am more powerless than when I was merely a landless noble at court. Every failure is a mark against me."

Before he could go on waxing poetic she interrupted. "And have they mentioned the French King?"

His eyes widened a fraction. "Have you set spies around me?"

"No. I don't need to. Joan was forthcoming with the information."

He gave a shake of his head. "And I thought you women did nothing but gossip and play cards."

"If that was a jest, I am not amused."

"Forgive me," he said, with a sigh. "I don't know what to make of it. They made compelling arguments, but I have my doubts. And my uncle Peter is bound to catch wind of what we are up to. He probably has spies all around us."

"He would be a poor advisor to your mother if he didn't. We must be careful. I worry that we are stepping into dangerous territory, but perhaps this is also our chance to make your parents listen. Enough is enough. They need to trust you with the men and money you need to manage Gascony."

"I know. I am open to discussing this more. Perhaps, my Lusignan uncles are right and I should deal with the French King directly. Perhaps some deal can be reached that would benefit us without making us traitors to England."

"It's a difficult ground we tread. Perhaps, through my mother in Ponthieu we can communicate with the French king circumventing the Lusignans altogether." She shifted so she could fit into the crook of his arm. His warmth was always a comfort to her. "Do you worry that I have not given you a child yet?"

All she could hear for a time was his steady breathing. Then he tilted her chin up.

"No. If anything I prefer that I don't have to share you with our little spawn. Nor do I enjoy the thought of you risking yourself. Our lives are complicated enough without adding a child to the mix."

"That is very rational of you. I cannot help but fear—"

He silenced her with a kiss. "I would be a poor knight indeed if I cannot chase away your fears. You have my devotion and admiration. At the moment I require nothing more. Later on, perhaps, it will be different."

"Once you are king?" she asked in a teasing tone.

"Certainly. The moment we are crowned I shall demand a nursery full of brats to ensure the safety of the succession."

"And if none come?"

Edward gave a small shrug. "I have brothers and sisters

enough. They shall be more than pleased to inherit after me. I have no doubt that is what they are praying for."

"But—"

He let out a heavy sigh. "I am your husband, am I not? You must learn to listen to me without question."

She laughed at his pompous tone and even more when his expression turned to shock.

"What is this, wife? Laughing at me? I cannot stand for this."

He sat up, which only made her laugh harder.

"Such disrespect," he said, clicking his tongue.

Her laughter was muffled by his heated kiss and all doubts fled away in the face of such assurances.

The household quickly adjusted to the newcomers. Permanent rooms were allocated to their Lusignan kin and they blended in well. It was important to both Edward and Eleanor that they had every comfort they could wish for.

In exchange, the three brothers acted as councilors to Edward. William and Guy often rode out with him when he journeyed around Gascony to settle disputes.

Having been so long on her own, Eleanor found she enjoyed having another woman in the household she could regard as more of an equal. When the weather permitted, they went out hawking or sat in the garden listening to the songs of French troubadours.

It was quite an idyllic arrangement.

By late summer, Joan had begun showing. As her belly

grew she increasingly confined herself to the keep, finding she had little energy for anything but mundane tasks.

"I am sorry I cannot come with you to the dairy today," Joan said. Her feet were elevated on a cushion. As she shifted, she winced.

"Are you alright?" Eleanor asked coming forward, filled with genuine concern.

"Of course. It's just the baby moving. Every great kick he gives me makes me lose my breath. But it's a pleasure to know he is growing strong."

"I shall have to speak to him once he is born. He shall have to ensure he repays you for all this pain he has caused you."

Joan smoothed a hand over her rounded belly. "I am sure he will repent, and I shall be quick to forgive him and spoil him rotten."

Eleanor touched her shoulder. "Well, I shall leave you to rest and will see you later. Send for me if you need anything. I am not going far."

Joan nodded, a distracted look in her eyes.

Eleanor left the solar, grateful she wasn't encumbered by a great belly.

She journeyed to the dairy to see that the new building had everything necessary. This had been one of her many projects for improving the castle. The old dairy had been too small to accommodate the growing population and was in desperate need of renovation.

Situated on the northern side of the keep, the dairy was built of heavy stone and brick. Whitewash and tiles decorated the walls and floors, allowing the area to be kept clean and free from any dirt or foul miasmas that might taint the milk and cheese produced.

Eleanor found the dairymaids hard at work, one churning butter while the others mixed rennet into milk.

"My Lady, welcome," the four maids said, bowing low, their movements unpracticed but genuine.

Eleanor smiled and bade them show her what they were working on, asking how they liked the improvements and what else they might require. Then she examined the store-rooms where rounds of hard cheese were kept, as well as butter and cheese. This room was dug deep into the ground where the earth kept it cool and helped keep everything fresh for longer. Come winter they would appreciate the cheese.

After a quick sample of the cream, Eleanor moved on to tour the rest of the castle, ensuring everything was as it should be. Any disputes among the household staff came to her. Edward had no time for what he saw as petty squabbles and trusted her to see to the household management. With the help of other key members, including the steward, chamberlain and marshal, she oversaw everything from the lamps in the sconces to the linen napkins, ensuring the castle was well stocked and efficiently run. At any moment they might be placed under siege, so managing the food and fresh water was imperative. If only the treasury was as well-kept as the rest of the household, at the moment, it was piti-fully empty.

As she rounded the corner she found Jasper, Edward's marshal and trusted comrade, waiting in an alcove. He caught her eye and bowed before falling into step as she walked towards the ramparts of the castle gates.

"My Lady, I have spoken to your husband about the need for weapons for the men. The situation is dire, and as yet, no action has been taken. There's only so many times their blades can be resharpened before they weaken and snap. My men are at a loss as their blades grow dull and our supply of arrowheads dwindles with each passing week."

Eleanor eyed him. It amused her that while Edward and his commanders believed she had no business making battle plans; they had no qualms turning to her for financing.

"My lord has been occupied," Eleanor said, gently reminding the marshal he was walking a fine line.

He checked himself. "There has been much on his mind, which is why I come to you, My Lady."

"What do you need? Do you have a list of the steel you need to craft these new weapons?"

They'd reached the bottom of the stairs and he motioned for her to go first.

"I have consulted with the blacksmiths and taken an inventory. We hoped the last delegation from England would bring the supplies we asked for from the King. But all we received were promises, and the blacksmiths can't fire up their furnaces with air alone."

"That would be a miracle," Eleanor said, sighing. Indeed, the last message from the King's council had refused Edward any more men and urged the Prince to curb his expenses. There was no mention of the Lusignans who had taken residence in their household, but this was clearly a punishment for the disrespect. It must have been Queen Alienor's doing.

"Winter is fast approaching, and it is likely we will have

peace, but it won't hold once the ice thaws. We must be ready for the spring."

"You always have an eye to the future," Eleanor said, as they finished their long climb and stood on the wall that overlooked the vast, flat plain surrounding the castle. No one could sneak up without being noticed. Below, the water in the moat reflected the sun, making it sparkle.

In the past, besieging armies had trampled the fields until there was nothing but dirt. Yet here was the land, restored to its verdant green. The cyclical nature of things comforted Eleanor.

A breeze buffeted her and she breathed deep. The fresh air filled her with courage and renewed her spirits.

"Give me a tally of what you need and I shall find the money. You are right — we need to prepare for what is to come. Being caught unprepared would be disastrous."

"There are some who would be willing to extend us credit," the marshal said, stumbling over his words. It took her a moment to realize he meant the Jewish moneylenders.

Many Christians were of the opinion it would be preferable to expel the Jewish people from England rather than allow them to prosper. They'd become entrenched in the kingdom, lending money at high interest rates. Many, including the King himself, were indebted to them.

Eleanor tapped her fingers on the jagged stone of the parapet. The idea of more debt made her stomach roil. She turned her head to the west, where England lay. No help was coming from that quarter.

"If matters become dire then of course we shall do all we can to avert disaster," she said, finding herself unable to commit to a course of action.

"As you wish, My Lady," the marshal said, bowing his head. "I shall send you the list." He turned to leave, but she stopped him.

"Should we need to call upon their aid, I don't — I don't wish for them to know to whom they are lending the money. My name and the Prince's must not be said in the same sentence."

"That is not—"

"It's my command," she interrupted, and spun to face him. "The English people grumble about us already. I will not add more kindling to the fire of my husband's demise. There are other ways that don't involve resorting to money-lenders."

"Like the French King?" he asked. The question was innocent enough, but Eleanor caught the rage that flickered across his face.

She stared him down. She wasn't the sort to quake in fear at the first hint of opposition or displeasure. "It is better if we cement strong alliances instead of burning away the goodwill of our people by going against the word of God. You shall have your weapons, but you cannot dictate how they'll be paid for."

He kneeled at her feet, as was proper, and asked for her forgiveness. "I spoke out of turn, My Lady. My worry is that this matter requires speed. We cannot prevaricate while the funds are found. If the French knew how weak we were, they would press their advantage."

"Then it behooves us to keep them from finding out." She laid her hands on his shoulder and bid him rise. "I know you are loyal and the French have been your enemy for far longer than they've been mine." She pulled at the sleeve of her gown, recalling the tract from Virgil she'd been translating. "The ideal solution would be peace. That is the only way to prosperity."

The marshal was silent and she knew that he, like many of the English, thought peace would only come when France was conquered and all Frenchmen were nothing but dust.

"Let me ask you. Is it better to negotiate while you still have power or after you've already lost?"

"Power. Obviously. But the French—"

"Aren't to be trusted. I know." She nodded her head sagely. "For now, though, I would prefer to know our borders are safe. Don't be angry with my husband for thinking that his only option is to negotiate with the French King. If he had it his way, he'd be leading the English army into France."

"His uncles influence him. That is what I'm concerned about," Jasper confessed in a whisper. "I can see the wisdom of your words but is it not suspicious that shortly after they took up residence here, our lord began talking about peace with France? They were exiled for a reason, and I cannot help suspect we are harboring vipers."

She gave him a sorrowful smile. Peter of Savoy had been hard at work filling their men's heads with lies and anxieties.

"The Lusignans are loyal to England. They came to us when they could've fled to the French court. You've seen them ride out on patrol. This would hardly be the work of people who wish to see us destroyed."

The marshal grunted.

She couldn't be sure if he believed her or not. Did it

matter, in the end? A smile spread across her features. "There's no use squabbling. Time will tell who is friend or foe. In the meantime we have work to do."

Chastened, he nodded and left without another word.

It worried her, this first hint of discord among their household. She looked over her shoulder one last time at the blue, cloudless sky and the green fields. Had it been a mistake to open their gates to Edward's uncles? Even she was beginning to have doubts. Not of their good intentions, rather because of the trouble they were causing for them.

She wished she had the power to divine the future, as the pagans had done when the Roman Empire was at its height and their priests and priestesses received the blessings of their false gods.

She knew matters were complicated. She'd been confident in her delivery of that pretty little speech to the marshal, but in truth, doubt gnawed at her. Was it worth the risk of negotiating with the French King, as Edward was keen to do? Had the Lusignans made some private deal with the French King? Would be lead to their mutual destruction?

She cracked her knuckles and walked away, determined to banish her bad mood, and soon found herself in her library and study — her sanctuary. She had paid carpenters to build shelves on which to keep the various scrolls, manuscripts and books she'd collected over the years. The smell of vellum, parchment and ink permeated the air.

It was just after midday, and sunlight streamed in through the stained-glass windows. This had once been a private chapel that had fallen into disrepair. Edward had allowed her to use it for her 'projects', as he liked to call them. He was a man of action and didn't value books as much as she did. But at least he humored her. In time, Eleanor believed he would come to appreciate the wisdom found on these pages. She deftly moved about the room, making sure everything was in its place.

She allowed no one in here, afraid that one careless servant with a candle would set the whole place ablaze. There were volumes from Castile, brought here from the Holy Land by her father.

In Castile, learning and education was prized as much as one's ability with a sword. England was different, and it had taken her time to adjust to its foreign customs and way of thinking.

Eleanor found comrades among the priests of the realm, but rarely did she find another among the nobility. Several lords kept small libraries and displayed them to distinguished guests, but they were for show. Many were barely literate. It was a shame.

With the priests, she found acceptance and appreciation, though she suspected that had more to do with all her generous donations than her knowledge. It didn't stop her from surrounding herself with scholars and encouraging her husband to be charitable to the monasteries.

When Joan had first arrived, Eleanor had shown her an Illyrian poem translated from that ancient language into Greek and then French. It was a beautiful piece of work, and she marveled at how the words of some ancient poet transcended to today.

The countess had made a great show of examining it, but it was clear she had no genuine passion for it. Disappointed, Eleanor came here by herself whenever she could slip away without being a neglectful host.

Now she sat at her crude desk and began reading Virgil. The effort of reading and understanding his words kept her mind focused and numb to all else. In moments like these, her worries slipped away.

An hour later, she exited her private library and made her way back to the women's quarters, ready to face the rest of the day. A dreamy smile spread across her lips.

CHAPTER 4

1259, GASCONY

Eleanor felt besieged by enemies. Peter of Savoy was still here, trying to impose his will on the country and stirring up trouble whenever he had the opportunity. Then there were the Lusignans, who were quickly taking her place in Edward's private council.

She didn't know how it happened, but little by little she was being excluded from his councils. It wasn't done maliciously, on Edward's part at least. But they could often go where she could not. She might follow behind on her mare during the hunt, but she was not in the thick of it. When they rode off to patrol the borders or chase down packs of robbers in the nearby forest, she was not with them.

If she had been with Edward more, she might have counseled him to tread carefully.

Now at last they were locked away together for a private meal. She craned her neck as a messenger came in. He was pale, and she suspected he brought bad news.

Edward's eyes flicked to him, his shoulders tensing. "What is it?" he snapped.

"I come from the King and Queen, My Lord," he said, his eyes darting around the room. Eleanor could tell he was afraid. He might be of an age with her husband, but Edward was tall, and in his growing fury, intimidating.

The messenger held out the sealed letter. It bore the seal of both King and Queen, and whatever was in it must have been of great importance.

Edward ignored him and instead turned back to his dinner, picking over the bones of the quail. A deafening silence descended until at last he deigned to speak.

"What does it say?" Edward said, motioning to the letter.

"I do not know, My Lord," the messenger said, with fear in his voice.

Deciding now was as good a time as any, Eleanor interjected. "Edward, he is merely the messenger. Your quarrel is not with him. My love, have pity on him, think of the long distance he has had to travel to get here."

"They shouldn't have sent a child to do a man's work then."

She fixed him with a look and he capitulated.

Eleanor watched as he tore the seal with the dagger he wore at his side and read the missive. His expression was indifferent, but Eleanor saw his grip on the parchment tighten.

Then he handed it to her before turning his attention back to the young messenger. "You will have your answer soon enough. Go and dine in my hall, for soon you shall find yourself back on the road."

The messenger looked relieved. He bowed respectfully before repeating the motion to Eleanor with gratitude in his expression.

Once they were alone, Edward smiled across the table at her. "I wouldn't be surprised if he's not half in love with you already."

Not wishing to be distracted from the matter at hand, she shrugged. "I've always told you a bit of kindness goes a long way."

"My temper got the better of me." Edward leaned back in his chair, watching her as she mulled over the letter.

It started off with the usual platitudes written in a stranger's hand, but then the script changed and her eyebrows arched. "Your sister Beatrice is betrothed and to leave for France soon?"

"They couldn't even get her a Prince. Only some Duke." Edward shook his head. "Read on."

Eleanor didn't have to be urged. Beatrice was Edward's younger sister, a demure but pretty creature. It was true she wouldn't have survived the complexities of the French court, but was throwing her away on the Duke of Brittany the answer? It made England seem weak. The letter went on to say that this marriage would cement a treaty with the French King, and that King Henry was prepared to relinquish the claims on several French provinces in exchange for peace. It wasn't clear if the French King would return the favor. Her mouth went dry as she saw the postscript written in the Queen's elegant handwriting.

You are to remain in Gascony and learn to obey your King and father. You have imperiled us all with your indiscretion. I shall pray for you to see the error of your ways.

Eleanor blanched. "What is she referring to?"

Edward set down his fork and threw his napkin on the plate. He paced around the room restlessly, running his hands through his hair, tormented by angry thoughts.

"One can only guess what lies my uncle has been telling her. I have been in communication with the French court trying to broker a treaty with them. I wasn't making overtures to the French King, but clearly my parents believe I am plotting against them. As a result, we aren't invited to my sister's wedding or to the meeting with King Louis. I am my father's heir, yet he seems content to cast me aside as if I was nothing more than his bastard son."

Aware of the servants in the room, Eleanor approached him and set her hand on his shoulder. "Peace, Edward. You shouldn't read into everything. Perhaps this was all a misunderstanding. If you write to your father, I am sure he will invite you to Paris. Of course, you should be there to sign the treaty."

Edward shook his head. "No. There's no use fighting it or begging for scraps. My own parents think I am a deceitful liar working against them. But why should I, when I stand to inherit everything? All I want is to safeguard the kingdom and continue to expand its borders. My father and mother are greedy cowards. They will not fight the French as they ought to. They are content to sign treaties if it means they can go on living in luxury in England. How could they believe the French will allow us to continue ruling Gascony, Limoges and Perigord? And how on God's good earth could my father exchange this for his claim on the rest of France? Normandy alone is worth twice Gascony. Are we not directly descended from the Dukes of Normandy? It is our destiny to be rulers of France and England. Yet he can give it up so easily. He's misguided at best and a coward at worst," he said, not caring who heard.

Eleanor felt her chest tighten even more, because she was quickly realizing she wasn't as aware of her husband's comings and goings as she'd thought.

Were the Lusignans to blame for this rift between them? She tried to ignore the disloyal thoughts.

"My Lord, nothing is set in stone. We must wait and see. Besides, your claims to those lands are just. Your only concern now should be how you will be a good lord to your people.

"Yes, yes," he growled. Then in a whisper added, "Why do they not trust me? How can they accuse me of such disloyalty? It breaks my heart."

"I know." Eleanor kissed his cheek. "Give it time."

But Edward would not be cautioned.

Furious at being excluded from the treaty negotiations, Edward wrote a scathing letter decrying his parents' eagerness to cast aside England's claim to France. Had they wished, they could've busied themselves with recapturing the lost English territories. Normandy had always been held by England. They couldn't, they *shouldn't* let it fall away.

He wrote to the English Parliament begging them to stop this madness. And he wrote to his parents promising his filial obedience, even as he cursed their weakness.

It did not matter what he did, his parents were eager to teach him a lesson and he was ordered to remain in Gascony.

The Lusignans were silent, but encouraged Edward as much as they dared. In spite of the friendship blossoming between herself and Joan, Eleanor hated their influence. They emboldened Edward to take more risk, but they didn't have everything to lose, while he did.

Joan's growing discomfort meant she increasingly kept to her chambers. Her belly had grown great, and Eleanor wondered if she was carrying twins.

"I hope not," Joan said with a strained laugh. "But it shall be as God wills it."

Eleanor made the sign of the cross. Every woman feared childbirth. The outcomes were often deadly for both mother and child. She'd seen how prayers and holy objects could be used to help ease the birth, but they did little to assuage the fear or pain.

Yet for all this, many women, herself included, prayed for the blessing of a child. There was plenty for Eleanor to do without worrying about a child, but England would need an heir to come after Edward. She wanted to give him all the sons and daughters he could want to safeguard his kingdom and his vision for the future.

Another, smaller part of her worried that in time, no matter how much they might love each other, she might be required to step aside and allow him to take a new wife. One who could give him children. The thought weighed heavily on her and so she prayed. These days Edward rarely came to her bed, even though they were often in each other's company.

Outside, heavy autumn rains pelted the ground and any poor creature daring the road. Eleanor watched from the oriel window.

"Shall I fetch you some hymns from my special library? They are in Latin but I could translate into French for you."

Joan looked up from her stitching to smile at her. "That would do me a world of good, but I wouldn't wish to trouble you."

"Nonsense," Eleanor said. "What else do I have to do?"

Joan grinned. "You're as busy as a bee. I don't know how you find the energy."

"I can't help myself," Eleanor said, surprised at her own confession. "I have to make myself useful. So allow me to be of some help."

"You could pick up the needle and help me sew this christening gown."

Joan had been straining her eyes sewing white stitches against the white linen. Despite claiming to be half-blind, they were still neater than Eleanor's would've been.

"I dare not, for despite my best intentions I would be sure to ruin it."

"Nonsense. It would be an honor to this future child to have something sewn by the future Queen of England."

"May that be a long time coming."

"Amen."

"But I shall think of something to give that little creature you are growing. Perhaps I shall embroider him a pillow. My talent is good enough for that."

As she selected some suitable fabric, she studied Joan more closely, wondering how to get her to divulge her hopes. "Will you return to England to give birth, or will you stay here? You are welcome either way."

Joan's needle never stopped moving. "If things were different I would've preferred my baby to be born in England. I have a castle of my own and one day this child of mine may inherit it. It's an old wives' tale perhaps, but they say it is good luck if the heir is born on the land he will one day inherit." She gave a shake of her head. "But it's all superstition. I inherited, and I was not born at Pembroke Castle."

Eleanor smiled kindly. "I wish with all my heart we'd been invited to Paris with the rest of the King's council. Do you know what our husbands have done to anger the King and Queen so much?"

Joan shook her head. "No. I know they wrote to the French King trying to broker their own terms with him before this new treaty came into being. William hasn't told me much but to be honest, I have been distracted. What do you think of it?"

"It's strange how quickly it came about. But we must rely on secondhand accounts here in Gascony."

"Would you return to England, Princess?" Joan asked.

"I would, but not as supplicants. Edward is the prince and heir. He shouldn't be treated like some villain. But regardless, it is pointless to wish for things to change. My only hope is that neither of our husbands take drastic action."

Joan nodded, but was preoccupied with her needlework.

The very king who had ordered her marriage was the same one who had exiled her. Women always suffered at the hands of men, regardless of what they did. Eleanor was determined to act as she saw fit. Then at least if she was exiled or sent away in shame, it would've been her doing and not Edward's.

"I shall go find that book. You will enjoy it, if all you've heard before is the English verse."

CHAPTER 5

1259-1260, GASCONY

"My love, I have something to show you."

Eleanor blinked away the sleep and, realizing Edward was at her bedside, shot up. "Are we under attack?"

He smiled. "I'd be coming to you in my armor if that was the case. No, but I need your advice, if you'd give it."

"Willingly." She rubbed her eyes — not the most dignified thing she could've done.

He pulled her out of her rooms past her sleeping ladies, who glanced up then lay back down once they saw it was Eleanor's husband leading her away. More than likely they were imagining the pair of them were fleeing to somewhere private, for a lovers' tryst.

Edward's mind was weighed down by more important matters. He held her hand gently enough as he pulled her along, but she was certain he wasn't taking her on some romantic adventure.

In the end, he pulled her into Robert's office. The room had been converted from a storeroom, but it was out of the way of the rest of the household, and private.

The Lusignan brothers were already there, and at the back of the darkened chamber was another man, cloaked in shadow.

Eleanor wasn't sure what to make of this; only Edward's reassuring presence kept her from panicking.

"My lords, now that we are all assembled, let us hear what Lord Simon has to say." Edward's voice was unwavering in its confidence.

Eleanor's gaze snapped to the stranger. Was this Simon de Montfort? It couldn't be. She fought to keep her expression passive.

It was then he stepped towards them and into the dim light of the candles lit sparingly around the room.

Simon de Montfort, the Earl of Leicester, had long been an enemy of the King and Queen. He opposed them in Parliament and stirred up discontent among the nobles. It was he who curbed Edward's allowance and refused the King permission to levy more taxes from his people. What could he want with them? Even as she considered the question, she suspected she knew. The scent of treason hung in the air, and it sent a shiver of apprehension down her spine.

"My lords, my lady." Simon bowed his head respectfully towards her. She merely inclined her head. Even at his age he was still a handsome man, well built and solid. His open expression and willingness to laugh made him approachable. Eleanor could sense he was a charismatic man and if she hadn't known better she might have found herself charmed by his disarming smile. It was no surprise he gathered such a large faction at court. "Thank you for agreeing to meet with me. I know this has been a trying time for everyone."

Guy scoffed, but William was watching Simon intently.

Simon had often spoken out in public against the Lusignan appointments, claiming they didn't deserve the honors bestowed upon them, and that they were bankrupting the kingdom with their greed.

Guy, who was more vindictive, crossed his arms in front of his chest and waited for Simon to beg for forgiveness. At least, that was how Eleanor read the situation.

Simon ignored Guy and addressed Edward directly.

"My Prince, I owe you my fealty. You must know how your people balk at your father's treaty with the French. Thousands of English lives have already been lost in the fight for France and now their sacrifice is to be for nothing? What do you think, My Lord, for I greatly wish to know your thoughts on this?"

Eleanor whipped around, ready to silence Edward, but he merely gave a shake of his head.

"The King is well meaning. He wants peace. As I'm sure, do we all," he said, his voice steady. "I will not dig my own grave by daring to share my opinion with my father's enemy. Do I trust the treaty will hold? Do I think the terms are fair? No, on both accounts. But I believe my father has the kingdom's best interests at heart. I wonder who has misled my father into thinking this was the best course of action."

Edward's words did not deter Simon, who merely smiled ruefully. "The English barons abhor the very thought of giving up our claim to Normandy, and the rest of the French provinces that rightfully belong to us. With your support, we could fight against this treaty and ensure it is not signed. As you say, someone must be misleading him into believing that such a thing would be good for the country. By all accounts he should be King of both England and France. Who could've convinced him to throw away his claim?" Simon spoke with such passion that even Eleanor, who was distrustful of him, found herself pulled in.

Glancing at Edward, she could see he was struggling with his own sense of morality. Privately he had expressed his hatred for the treaty, but did he dare speak out against his father? And to the likes of Simon de Montfort?

Now they had to consider who stood to benefit from the King taking such a drastic step?

There was only one person in the kingdom with the power to influence him, and every person in this room knew who it was. Queen Alienor, who had always favored her French relatives so highly and cared more for her wealth and jewels than for England.

No one said it, but as they regarded each other it was plain enough on their faces that they knew.

"I was trying to broker some arrangement with King Louis," Edward said, as though confessing. "The terms of such a peace would not have been to abandon our claims to the French throne. I am left to hold Gascony without money nor men. You can see for yourself, Lord Simon, that I keep a modest household. I do not parade around in jewels and I have not draped my wife in the silks and diamonds that ought to belong to her. Her revenues from Ponthieu go directly to the war effort. They buy us food, weapons, and when possible, peace. I have petitioned Parliament several times for funds and men. Yet my desperate pleas fall on deaf ears."

Simon bowed his head, for he had been one of those who struck down the request. Eleanor was pleased that Edward had all but named his price without saying anything overtly. Even his onetime nemesis could appreciate this.

"It is true, my Prince. I won't make a liar of myself by claiming otherwise. What I heard led me to misunderstand the situation. Now that I'm here, I can see for myself how tenuous the situation in Gascony is and equally how dedicated you are to keeping it in English hands. Rumors of your excess and frivolity made me doubt your need. I apologize."

Simon de Montfort's cordiality surprised Eleanor. But he wasn't some young man with something to prove. By now he was a seasoned politician and warrior.

Edward regarded him closely.

It was hard for Eleanor to read him, and usually she had a good sense of people. On the other hand, what choice did they have?

"Do you suspect there's more to this treaty than the settling of disputes over the French and English borders?" Eleanor asked. It felt as though she hadn't spoken in days, and she sounded timid and unsure.

Simon's eyes snapped to hers, seeing her as though for the first time. Indeed, until this moment his scrutiny had been reserved for Edward. Feeling the weight of his gaze, she shifted from one foot to another.

"I fear there is a deal being conducted behind closed

doors and this is merely a pretense. Who knows what clauses are hidden in the treaty," he said, levelly.

The others sucked in their breath; Eleanor could see the question on their lips but she didn't need Simon's answer to guess what this was really about.

She closed her eyes as she took a steadying breath. "You fear King Henry will ask for King Louis' help against the Barons now ruling Parliament." She cocked her head to the side. "You are no longer trusted or needed as much as you once were in England."

"You have an astute understanding of things, My Lady," Simon said, neither confirming nor denying her words. "I fear that the King will find some way to revoke the promises he made at the Parliament of 1258."

"And you come to me?" Edward laughed.

"I believe we have much to gain from each other. I do not question your father's right to rule, but he is a man whose power should be kept in check. No one but God should have endless power. You see for yourself how suspicious your father grows of you. How he casts aside his own kin."

There was a murmur of agreement among the men, but Eleanor caught William's glance and the way his lips thinned for the slightest moment. He, at least, did not forget that at one time Simon was their enemy and had played a key role in casting them out into exile.

"We must work together to prevail against the forces that set your father and my king to work against the best interest of his kingdom. We do not need to bow to France or go to them for aid. It's an insult."

Edward, with his deep sense of pride, nodded in agreement.

"We have much to discuss, then. Will you not take a seat?"

Until this moment they'd been standing around like conspirators and enemies, unsure if they should embrace each other or attack, but Edward had made his decision.

As Eleanor retreated to a stool by the far wall to watch the proceedings, she wondered if this was the right decision. However, the King and Queen had left them with little choice. They couldn't be allowed to go on while their personal greed and ambition destroyed the country.

As the four men began laying down the foundation of what would become their truce, Eleanor observed them in silence. From time to time she felt their attention drift to her but she wasn't invited to speak. Now that she was married, Ponthieu would theoretically pass on to her husband, but she would still be its de facto ruler. As incredulous as it might seem, there was always the chance she would refuse to raise her levies or support her husband.

Eleanor would never be so disloyal as to do that. It appeared that Simon had no such scruples and was willing to make alliances that suited him. Perhaps he saw hope for a future in which Edward sat on the throne. Unlike his father, Edward was steadfast and smart. While he had a good heart and thought of his people, he was also politically minded and didn't overreach himself.

Even this very meeting demonstrated that Edward wasn't petty.

On the other hand, Simon had once been the enemy of

both her husband and the Lusignans. Would the peace between them truly hold?

And what would happen if Edward's parents found out about this meeting? Eleanor shut her eyes as if to keep away the dark thoughts threatening to overwhelm her.

As she'd often done as a child when she felt nervous or frightened, she made herself smile. In this way she kept the anxieties at bay.

"You are welcome to stay here as our guest, Lord Simon," Edward said.

"As much as my old bones would appreciate the offer, I must be gone from here before I am noticed. You have given me much to think about. Thank you for meeting with me," he said, bowing to Edward and bidding the others farewell. To Eleanor he was far more attentive. "I believe your husband is lucky to have you. I hope he shows you all the honor you deserve."

"Thank you," she said, tilting her head in acknowledgement of the compliment.

Once he was gone the men returned to the room. Guy shot a glance her way.

"Ought your lady not retire for the night while we discuss what we should do?" Guy asked.

Eleanor felt herself straighten at the indignation of such a question. Edward silenced him with one look.

"So gentlemen, what is your opinion? Shall we trust him?"

"He has just as much to lose from this meeting as we do. I believe for once our goals align and as long as they do, he will hold true," William said.

"I agree," Eleanor threw in for good measure, silencing Guy who'd been ready with some reminder of Simon's past treachery. "His position is tenuous and he needs us if he wishes to maintain some level of legitimacy among the English people. He'd hate to be known as a usurper."

"He will be loyal until he feels secure again. After that, who knows?" Bishop Aymer said, taking a seat on one of the high-back chairs and leaning back with a grunt. As a child, he'd fallen off a horse and suffered pains in his back ever since. It was tragic how one small accident could change a life forever. If not for that, he might have been a great warrior and commander, like his older brother.

"Then we must prepare for this alliance to be of short duration," Edward said. "In the meantime we can enjoy its fruits and strengthen our own position."

They spoke until the first signs of dawn, and only then did they retreat to their beds.

In October, Parliament granted Edward a sum of four hundred pounds to strengthen his position and purchase the supplies he would need for the upcoming spring, when fresh conflicts in Gascony were sure to pop up.

In exchange, Edward wrote Parliament another lengthy letter outlining why he opposed this treaty with France. While the letter was carefully worded, stating that he was a loyal subject and would cleave to his parents' wishes, this was the first time he had openly spoken out against them so directly.

In the end, it did little good. Regardless of how Simon de Montfort, Edward and Parliament raised objections to the terms of the treaty, the King was resolute in pursuing it. Heavily guarded, the royal couple and Beatrice left for France where they were invited to stay with King Louis.

Edward was in a terrible mood all that fall, and even with the Christmas season upon them, he couldn't bring himself to smile at the entertainments Eleanor had arranged.

Shortly after the news that the Treaty of Paris was officially signed in December, Joan went into confinement.

Eleanor made a point of visiting her every day, and ensured she had both enough food and entertainment to keep her from becoming bored. The mood was lighter in that darkened chamber, with ladies praying day and night for the safe delivery of the Countess of Pembroke, than out in the great hall where the men huffed with indignation. Indeed, Edward had been privately castigated by his parents for stepping out of turn and allowing himself to be led astray.

It infuriated him.

News reached them that the French Dauphin and heir to the crown died, and mourning dictated that the marriage of Beatrice to John, Duke of Brittany, be postponed. Back in England, the mood was growing dangerous. Public opinion soured against the absent King and Queen.

No true Englishman wished to become a subject of France, and the way their monarchs were leaning on the French King for support rankled their pride. The barons were just as outraged and made overtures to Simon, hoping he would return to govern them. The atmosphere was tense, so it came as no surprise when King Henry announced his diminished court would spend Easter in Saint-Omer.

Shortly before Christmas Day, Joan's pains began. Eleanor attended her throughout the long night, encouraging her and sponging her forehead with cool water until at last the babe was born.

Joan, weak and exhausted from her travail, cried as she beheld her child. A son. From his demanding cries and the way he kicked when he was un-swaddled, it seemed he was strong and healthy.

William was overjoyed, and the proud parents praised every little thing their son did. They decided to christen him Aymer.

Eleanor and Edward stood as godparents, while the child was baptized by his namesake.

"He screams an awful lot," Edward said, though he was smiling down at the infant.

"You would too if you were dunked into a basin of cold water," Eleanor said, unable to keep from defending the poor soul.

"It's the Devil leaving him — or at least that's what my confessor said to me after I witnessed one of my sister's baptisms."

"How old were you?"

"Eight? Or there about."

"What a terrible thing to say to a child. I believe all children come into this world innocent. It's only as they grow that they learn to sin."

"It's a hard world." Edward drifted away from her as she held the now sleeping babe in her arms.

She looked down at his peaceful expression and wondered what was bothering Edward.

Little Aymer was returned to his mother, along with rich gifts befitting the future Earl of Pembroke. There were bolts of rich blue damask and linen embroidered along the hem with the Pembroke coat of arms, as well as other trinkets. Eleanor had also commissioned a beautiful gold crucifix and a chalice made of pure silver, which she buffed until it shone.

"You spoil him," Joan said with a happy little sigh as she sank back into her pillows. It had been two weeks since she'd given birth, but she was still recovering. Soon she'd be churched and Eleanor wondered if she'd be well enough to stand.

"He deserves to be spoiled," Eleanor said. "Besides, I'm practicing for when I have one of my own."

Joan shifted on the bed and the movement left her wincing. Concerned, Eleanor sent the maid to summon a midwife.

"You didn't have to," Joan said.

"There must be something they can do for you," Eleanor said, feeling uneasy at Joan's continued struggle to recover.

A little laugh escaped Joan. "I knew that giving birth was painful, but I wasn't prepared for what came after. Still, I must thank God I was safely delivered. The risk of childbed fever is gone by now. I just need to be patient."

Eleanor opened her mouth to protest, but the midwife had arrived looking irritated.

"What is it, My Lady?" she asked. Her tone was kindly enough, but the frustration was evident on her features.

"It was I who summoned you, Mistress Mary," Eleanor said, stepping in. "Can we not do something for her pain?"

The midwife clucked in disapproval. "Pain is woman's punishment for tempting Adam to sin. But let me examine you," she said, turning back to Joan.

After a quick examination, she decided Joan would benefit from a draught of mugwort and peppermint brewed together over a slow fire. "And plenty of rest. Don't get up."

She shuffled out of the room with an air of displeasure and haughtiness that had both Eleanor and Joan laughing.

"Why do I feel like I'm being lectured? Am I not the mistress here?" Eleanor shook her head, incredulous.

"Does she think I sneak out of this room to go riding? I have no inclination to ever leave this bed," Joan added, stifling a yawn. Much like her baby sleeping nearby, she needed to rest.

"I shall get out of your hair," Eleanor said, and went in search of her husband.

He was in the training yard, sparring with one of his men at arms. She watched from the side as the two men danced around each other, testing each other's defenses with wooden blades.

Edward feinted left and caught his opponent unaware. The man parried but tripped and fell to his knee. He surrendered as the next sword stroke fell.

Her husband clapped him on the back and helped him to his feet.

Eleanor chose that moment to come forward. "My Lord, well done."

"Thank you," he said, grinning from ear to ear.

"Do you have a moment to spare for me?"

"Always, my love." He leaped over the short fence of the tilting yard and took her hand in his. "Is all well?"

"Yes. I didn't mean to trouble you, but you've been distant lately and I wondered what was troubling you."

He brought her hand to his lips and placed a chaste kiss there.

"I forget how astute you are at reading my moods," he said, running a hand through his hair. He was still breathing hard from the exertion of sparring. "I've been accused of vile things. I fear my father will believe them."

Eleanor stopped in her tracks. "What?"

"Across the channel they say I am setting up a faction against my father. That I plan to take the throne from him in the Spring."

She gasped, then clasped her hand over her mouth to keep the sound from traveling further. "You cannot be serious. Edward — what shall we do?"

"Be calm, my love. It's all rumors. I have enemies a plenty who would love to see me pulled down. And many others who would love to see the kingdom destabilized."

She blinked, mulling over his words. "You don't mean King Louis, do you?"

Edward shrugged. "I have no proof of course, but it would suit his purpose, wouldn't it? As revenge for opposing the French treaty."

Eleanor bit back an unladylike curse.

Edward drew her close to him, his forehead resting on hers. "We are besieged by enemies, but we knew this."

"So now we must fight."

"Yes. Are you with me?"

"Of course." She smiled coyly up at him. "You are a renowned commander."

"Don't tease me, wife," he said.

"I'll tease if it puts a smile on your face."

Not caring who saw, she leaned up and kissed him on the lips.

CHAPTER 6

1260 - 1261, GASCONY

Time slipped through Eleanor's fingers. They went through the motions of celebrating Easter but their minds were focused on matters of war. Spring had marked the beginning of the campaigning season and Edward rode out with his men to patrol Gascony's borders. Any incursion on their lands was met with swift retaliation. They couldn't afford to show weakness.

Both Eleanor and Edward wrote beseeching letters to Parliament, reporting that the French were already breaking the terms of the treaty they had signed.

In exchange, Parliament reprimanded Edward for the attacks he led in French territories. They blamed him for disrupting the peace. It was an outright lie, but it was telling that his parents believed the French King rather than their own son.

Outrage spurred Edward on; he wouldn't back down, and he would muster as many men as he could to defend

Gascony. If he had been a proud man before, he was even prouder now.

Eleanor hoped this wouldn't consume him, but if anything, it emboldened him.

Every success, every victory gave him more confidence and won him the admiration of his men.

Simon de Montfort honored his end of the bargain and kept them abreast of news from England. It was through him that Eleanor was warned that the Queen had pawned some of her jewels.

Edward had ridden south when the messenger arrived, and she broke the seal herself.

My Lord Prince,

I hope this letter finds you well. I have discovered a plot your parents and their adherents are concocting. They plan to raise an army and pay for French mercenaries to come fight against me and my supporters. Jewels from the Queen's coffers are disappearing at an alarming rate. I fear they will move against us soon. What will become of England if we invite French armies in? Your parents will send someone to prevail upon you to give up your alliance with me. I pray that you do not. In my heart, all I want is for England to prosper and to protect it against unlawfulness.

S

By the time Eleanor had finished reading the letter, her heart was pounding. The pieces on the chessboard were moving and she felt they were too far from the center of power to make a difference.

She hurried to find Sir Robert Leyburn, to see if a messenger could be sent to Edward with all haste. He needed to be prepared. Who knows, his parents might even have him arrested. The thought alone caused her chest to tighten. Would they send an army to destroy their own son? The idea wasn't as farfetched as she would have liked. They had already banished him for a far lesser offence than speaking out against their policies. How she wished she could wield a sword herself. She'd do anything to protect Edward, but at the moment she felt powerless.

Why were his parents so determined to cast him as a villain when all he wished was to be a chivalrous knight and defender of the realm? They were fools.

And for the first time, Eleanor found herself wishing that her husband was indeed planning to usurp the throne.

Robert Leyburn was investigating the state of the kitchens when she came upon him at last.

"Princess," he said with a polite bow. "How may I assist you?" Already he could tell there was some fresh trouble. He looked exhausted. They all did.

Eleanor forced herself to smile and pretend nothing was wrong. Even with this trusted servant of theirs, she didn't dare reveal her concerns or the contents of this letter.

"Has there been any news from Prince Edward? I wish to send him a letter as soon as possible."

"Nothing new. If you give me the letter I will do so at once by the fastest messenger I have."

Eleanor nodded. "Thank you for your discretion. It is important he receives it. I shall reward the messenger with a gold coin if he performs his job well."

"With an incentive like that he might learn to fly," Sir Robert said. He didn't ask where she'd find the gold coin, for the treasury was looking bare these days.

Secreting herself in her private chamber, she pulled out

the personal book of hymns she carried on her girdle and began to translate her letter into the code Edward and she had devised in the early days of their marriage. You could never trust your letters. Seals could be opened, but it was harder to break a code. Edward had the exact same copy and he carried it in his breastplate even into battle. It'd become a memento between them. A good luck charm against the evils of the world. Now it would ensure she could communicate with him without anyone knowing.

After she watched the messenger ride off, the letter tucked safely in his saddlebags, she retreated to the interior of the keep. As always she had to wait. Patience was not her strong suit, and in an effort to keep herself busy she went to see Joan.

In her own apartments, Joan sat sewing with her women while her son, Aymer, was rocked in his crib. Now that he was five months old it was getting hard to keep him happy.

"And how is his lordship this afternoon?" Eleanor asked, standing over his crib.

"He's fussy," the nursemaid said. "I think another tooth is coming in."

"I'll have to ask the carpenter if he can make him a teething ring," Eleanor said, placing her hand on his little cheek. He gurgled up at her with the incoherent babbling of a babe.

Joan walked over grinning. "He's kept us up day and night. I hope he doesn't disturb you."

"The walls of the keep are thick, so no. I haven't had the pleasure of being awoken by his cries."

A smile broke across Joan's features. "I wish my husband could take it with such good humor as you do. I'm afraid he was far too eager to volunteer to go with Prince Edward to quell the unrest in the south."

"He's bored here. There's nothing to occupy a man like him."

"Perhaps." Joan looked to the side.

Eleanor reached for her hand and gave it a squeeze. "Trust me. He's as in love with you as ever. And I've never seen such a doting father before. He's as often in your son's nursery as he is training with his men."

"You are right. There is just so much uncertainty. I hate it. I thought my child would've been born in England. That I would have my lands restored to me and not be living off others' generosity. What will become of my son if we fail?"

"He will be loved. Many children can't claim to even have that. We see plenty of urchins wandering like wild animals in the city. Something ought to be done for them. They are without anyone to look after them."

Joan leaped at that thought. "Why, that is an excellent idea. I shall write to the Cistercian nuns at the Abbey of Sainte-Marie de Boulaur. Perhaps, they could take them in and give them an education. Those children deserve a chance at a better life. The Lord knows that war has created orphans in the both kingdoms. It breaks my heart to think of it."

"It is a noble cause worthy of our attention. It should provide us with plenty to do while the men pursue our enemies across the countryside."

They set to work outlining their plans, the estimated number of orphans and the funds that would be required for such an undertaking.

Eleanor received no reply to her letter to Edward. The messenger had returned and swore on the Bible that he had received it.

"I placed it into his hands myself, Lady," he said, on bended knee.

"I believe you. And yet he gives me no message? Has he said when he will return?"

He shook his head, looking despondent that he didn't have better news to bring her.

Impatience flared within her again, and it was only Joan's gentle prodding that pulled her away from the window, where she stood staring out at the courtyard, day in and day out.

On the fifth day, as Joan and Eleanor were penning out their proposal to the Cistercian nuns, trumpets sounded, announcing Edward's return.

Eleanor ran to greet him.

Once again forgoing all decorum, he pulled her into his arms and kissed her deeply. The gathered men applauded. They had grown to revere Edward for his prowess and bravery on the battlefield. He was a King Arthur straight of the sonnets, and she was his Guinevere, albeit with no plans to create discord by falling in love with one of his knights.

"I've missed you," he whispered once he pulled away.

"I, as well. I've prayed for your return for many days now. You received my message did you not?"

"I did. I'm afraid my father and mother are already sending over that delegate to entreat me to stop plotting against the King and ask for their mercy. It's ridiculous. But we must be ready to greet such an important visitor whenever they arrive, with all honor and respect."

She let out a long breath. Frustration was bubbling inside of her; it was growing hard to keep herself in check.

"It's good to be back," he said, sensing she needed to be distracted. "I'm famished. I don't remember the last time I had a decent meal."

She led him inside, placing her hand in the crook of his arm. "Perhaps, if you stayed at home more often, then you wouldn't suffer so."

"I'll keep that in mind."

While she entertained the returning soldiers with food and music, she anticipated the moment when Edward could slip away from the crowd and they would have the chance to speak in private.

When it came, they retreated to her chambers, but rather than fall into each other's arms, they fell into chairs before the fire and planned what the coming days would look like.

"Whoever my parents send, I am sure they will come with a summons for me to return to England. I am loath to leave Gascony, but I have prepared my commanders for such an eventuality. I trust both Jasper and Robert to hold the peace. They won't let it fall into French hands."

"And what about me? Will I be coming with you?" Eleanor asked. She knew she ought to go visit Ponthieu. It was overdue, but events being what they were she'd been unable to visit for years now.

"Let us see. If they ask for you to come then we will have no choice but I'd feel even better knowing you were here safeguarding our borders and maintaining our presence here. If the French believe we've abandoned Gascony they will pounce."

Eleanor nodded, unsure of what she hoped for now. "It sounds like we have a lot to consider." She let out a sigh and reached for her husband. "It feels like we never get more than a few stolen moments to be in each other's company."

"I promise everything shall change soon. My father must see reason. Perhaps, it would be a good thing if I were to return to England. I've been gone for too long. They must see me as a stranger who has forgotten all filial duty."

A royal messenger arrived at the beginning of June. The Earl of Gloucester, of all people, appeared at their doorstep with a large armed retinue, as though he feared being attacked.

"My Lord," Edward said, greeting him with what could only be called a strained smile. "You are most welcome, but surely bringing so many men was unnecessary. Though if this is a prelude to an invasion of Toulouse, I am eager to gather up my own force."

"My Prince." Gloucester bowed his head but didn't dismount from his horse. "I fear rumors have grown so great of your disobedience to your parents that I came here expecting all manner of treachery."

"You did?" Edward put a hand over his chest in mock

surprise. "It always astounds me how my actions get twisted. I am nothing if not a loyal subject."

"Your honored parents fear you work against them."

Anger flashed across Edward's features and Eleanor chose that time to step forward and interject. Gloucester, being older and a loyal adherent to King Henry, hated Edward, who he saw as a mere disobedient pup who needed to learn his place. He seemed to forget that one day Edward would be King. Perhaps his intense dislike overwhelmed his reason. He should consider being more respectful to Edward.

"We are greatly distressed to hear that his parents would think so," she said. "Please come inside. You are an honored guest. We would like to discuss these issues at length and reassure you and their graces of our utter love and devotion."

Edward muttered something under his breath that sounded an awful lot like a curse. Eleanor pinched him and subtly nudged him.

"As my wife says, you are welcome here. Please let us speak inside. Your men are welcome to join the feast. The tables are not as opulent as you might expect of a Prince of England, but you will find I am willing to make sacrifices to ensure I have the means with which to protect Gascony."

Gloucester relented and slid from his horse with a grunt he tried to disguise by snapping at the groom who stepped forward to lead away his horse.

The Earl was fifteen years Edward's senior, and at one time had been a ruthless warrior and commander. The years had withered away much of his strength, leaving behind an angry and cantankerous man who had aged before his time. It was no wonder he regarded a man like Edward with bitterness.

Nor did it help that Edward, being a prince, was not willing to back down and frequently argued with him.

Had King Henry sent Gloucester on purpose to annoy Edward? Was he really so guileless as to not understand that Gloucester was the last person he ought to send to negotiate a peaceful accord with Edward?

Remembering her role as hostess and the need to mediate between the two men, Eleanor shook herself out of her stupor.

She approached him with a smile. "My Lord, you must tell me your favorite dish and I shall have the kitchens make it for you."

He bowed respectfully to her. "I do enjoy venison. But I don't know what scrawny creatures Gascony can scrounge up."

Eleanor strained not to show her annoyance and in a good humor said, "At least the wine is good, My Lord. Come, let us get out of the sun."

With that they retreated inside.

The days following the Earl's arrival were tense. Guy was eager to show his displeasure by making himself scarce. What the Earl thought of this was unclear; perhaps he believed the Lusignans were scared of him and had gone off to hide.

William, the bravest of the three brothers, was keen to go about his business as though nothing was amiss.

It soon became apparent that wherever Edward went, Gloucester was not far behind.

"He's like a dog," Joan whispered under her breath,

chuckling. They had taken little Aymer out into the court-yard to enjoy the warm weather.

Eleanor was far from amused. "He's more like a farmer's dog making sure he keeps the herd together. I fear he will herd us back to our pen in England."

"You would miss Gascony so much?"

"I have nothing against England. But if we go now, we will be leaving behind the freedom we've enjoyed here. I shudder to think what sort of welcome we would receive at court. What has Peter of Savoy been telling them?"

Following Gloucester's arrival, Peter had left Gascony. He claimed the Queen had summoned him, but he couldn't produce the letters to prove it. Edward had been keen to forbid him and leverage this as proof of his treachery, but Eleanor had intervened. They would have gained nothing by forcing him to stay. The Queen and King were just as likely to take Peter of Savoy's side over their son's. Not wishing to invite further trouble by challenging him directly, they let him go.

On the second week after his arrival, Gloucester formally gave Edward a letter from his parents demanding he return to England with Eleanor in the hope that the family could reconcile and eliminate the discord between them.

Eleanor knew she would be leaping from one boiling pot to another. But they had no choice but to obey the summons.

They packed up their possessions in ox carts, and the castle was stripped of most of its finery. They would leave Gascony in the capable hands of Robert and Jasper.

The Lusignans were allowed to return temporarily, and

although there was no news of whether or not Joan's lands would be returned to her, she was still ecstatic to make the journey.

"I would've thought you'd be worried about Aymer crossing the channel," Eleanor teased, watching Joan humming while she packed away a trunk for her son.

"No harm will befall him. A little sea voyage doesn't scare me," she said with confidence. Then she paused, and glanced at Eleanor. "But we won't sail unless the weather is fair, correct?"

"Of course. I apologize — I didn't mean to cause you any anxiety. Just the other week you were worried about taking him into the gardens lest a bee sting him."

Joan laughed. "I forgot. The thought of England chases away all my fears. He belongs there."

"Eventually everything will be as it should be. You must have faith."

"I do." Joan looked resolute. "Just as I know in my heart that one day you and your husband's reputation will be restored."

Eleanor shrugged. As long as they survived, she no longer cared what King Henry and Queen Alienor thought of them. Eventually Edward would take the throne and they would be masters of their own destiny. They would show the world they were just rulers. "God willing," she said, though it was more a promise to herself than a prayer.

The King and Queen were in Kent, far from London where the people were sympathetic to Edward. Strange as this development was, by now Eleanor wasn't surprised by anything they did. Perhaps they even had an army standing around to protect them from their only son.

For all her misgivings, the signs were good that Edward's parents truly wished to reconcile with him. When they landed at Dover, rich gifts were waiting for them. Eleanor received new gowns and a beautiful bay mare, while Edward was gifted a gold chalice and a mantle of blue velvet stitched with England's lions in gold thread.

Their small party processed further into Kent, moving quickly. They had taken only the necessities with them, knowing their other belongings would follow behind in the slower ox carts.

Edward took care with his appearance as they rode through the towns, and people lined to road to watch him ride past. He was dressed in a leather jerkin with a cream silk shift beneath, and there was a simple sword in its scabbard at his belt. He looked every bit the dashing warrior prince. Nothing he wore was extravagant, and apart from his gold crucifix. Given the disgruntled mood of the populace, and how overtaxed they were, his coming must have felt like a breath of fresh air. Hope was rekindled that the Prince would liberate them from the oppression of his father.

Eleanor took care to dress just as plainly. The last thing she wanted was to be seen as a greedy. She wore a simple red silk dress, a plain gold band on her finger, and a rosary that hung from her leather girdle.

Along the way she stopped whenever she could to speak to the locals, offering kind words and throwing coins to beggars.

The people's affection for their prince became more genuine and they shouted blessings at them as they rode on through. When their way was blocked by a cart with a broken spoke, they stopped to assist. Edward himself rolled up his sleeves and helped his men lift the cart so the wheel could be removed and repaired.

That evening as they were preparing to sleep, Eleanor helped rub ointment into his blistered hands.

"Leave it alone, my love," he said. "They will become calluses in time. A man's hands ought not to be smooth and pretty like a woman's."

"You aren't like other men. You are a prince of this realm and one day you shall be king."

"Working in the hot sun today reminded me of the simple satisfaction working with one's hands can bring. It was much more enjoyable than this parading about wondering what everyone thinks of me."

She placed a gentle kiss on his lips. "You've done well. It is good for the people to remember that not everyone in the royal family is selfish. The barons rail against your parents for their excesses and portray themselves as the saviors of this nation. We must show everyone there is an alternative."

"Even if my family were to be overthrown, the barons would quickly turn on each other, vying for supremacy. By the end of the year, one of them would crown themselves King. I know that Simon de Montfort wishes to see England governed differently, but it will never happen. Not within our lifetimes. If ever."

Eleanor sat up, studying her husband's features more

closely. "Has he spoken to you about these reforms? Is that his price for supporting you in Gascony?"

Edward's lips curled into a smug smile. "Oh, he all but asked for the moon. But I agreed to support some of his demands. We are allies but we aren't friends. The loyalty that binds us is fragile. I daresay we will give up the alliance altogether the moment it no longer suits us."

"That sounds awfully cold of you, and unchivalrous."

"He's a powerful man with ambitions. We might be friends now, but he will turn on me."

"And if you are wrong?"

Edward shook his head. "I'm not wrong. Simon wants to be king in all but name. I know men like him."

Eleanor arched a brow and he grinned up at her. "I am one of those men. There is nothing I wouldn't do to ensure I am crowned. The only difference between Simon and myself is that I had the luck to be born the son of a King."

"And once you have England, will you be satisfied with that?" She reached over and ran her fingers through his golden hair.

"There's France to consider. That kingdom was nearly ours at one time. It slipped through our fingers. If I can, I will find a way to claim it. Then we will be a great empire. Greater than the Holy Roman Empire that stretches from the Northern sea to encompass Italy."

"Such ambitions," she said, laying her head down in the crook of his arm.

"Tell me — does the thought of such greatness not thrill you too?"

Her fingers splayed across the expanse of his chest. She

could feel the beat of his heart against her palm. It seemed to beat in tandem with hers. They were of one mind. "It does."

CHAPTER 7

1261, ENGLAND

They were greeted with all the pomp and ceremony they might have expected to receive as Prince and Princess of England, but there was a coolness in the greeting.

Many of the nobles gathered in the presence chamber to watch the family reunion avoided their gaze. Eleanor couldn't help noticing Peter of Savoy lurking at the back of the room, amusement dancing across his features.

The King and Queen were seated formally on thrones, with the cloth of estate hanging over them. They both wore their crowns and were richly decked in jewels and gold chains.

Eleanor felt like a pauper approaching the dais.

Along with Edward, she curtseyed low and remained in place until the King bid them rise.

Silence descended upon the gathering as the King

considered his son for what felt like an eternity. The Queen placed a hand on his forearm and he broke out of his reverie. As King Henry stepped down from the dais, he held out his arms in welcome to his son.

The two men embraced.

Then Edward dropped to his knees before his father and begged for his forgiveness. Despite the words of penance, he spoke without shame.

"Father, I am your loyal son and would never dream of disappointing you by going against your wishes. Long have I admired and respected you. I wish for nothing but peace between us and for us to understand one another. Many have tried to destabilize this realm with falsehoods. But here I come, your loving son, ready to do your bidding and ask for your forgiveness for any offense I may have caused you." As he fell silent, his words echoed around the chamber.

King Henry was moved to tears, and clasping his son by his shoulders, he bid him rise to his feet.

"We shall have peace between us," he declared and embraced him once more.

Polite applause from the watching court filled the air and Eleanor felt her attention drift to Queen Alienor, whose expression was as cool as it had been the moment they had entered.

It was she they would have to convince, and even then, Eleanor doubted Alienor would ever truly forgive them. The Queen was a patient woman with a taste for vengeance. Even if she didn't find some way to punish them now, she would in the coming months, or even years.

With the formality of the meeting over, the court slowly

retreated to the great hall where a wonderful feast had been prepared to welcome them.

Eleanor sat on Queen Alienor's left. She couldn't help noting that the cloth of estate appeared to have been altered since the last time she had dined here. No longer did it cover her; it barely touched her, as though Eleanor wasn't worthy of the honor. As if Eleanor wasn't royal and a future countess in her own right.

Still, she bore the insult with forbearance.

"It has been an age since I've last seen you, Queen Mother," Eleanor said, as platters of mutton cooked in red wine with stewed plums were placed before them. She served Alienor, as was polite, and then waited for her to speak. When she did not, Eleanor merely went on speaking as though nothing was wrong.

"The voyage was peaceful enough. Sir Royce is a fine sea captain. I must commend you for sending him to see us safely ashore," she said, her smile wide as she dished food onto her own plate and dug in. "This is delicious. I don't believe we have cooks half as good in Gascony. Secretly, I am so pleased we've returned to your court. It is good for a family to be together like this. Tell me, how was Princess Beatrice? She must be so happy to be settled into her own home now. The last time I saw her she talked of nothing else but wishing to be married—"

"Enough," Queen Alienor snapped.

Eleanor bent her head over her plate, hiding her satisfaction at having goaded her into acknowledging her presence. Then looking at her mother-in-law with wide eyes she placed a hand over her heart.

"I apologize if I have offended you, Your Grace."

"You need not prattle on so much. We both know you aren't some ignorant fool. Tell me how it came to be that my son would defy us? We trusted him with Gascony and he repays us with treachery."

"What do you mean?" Eleanor said, feeling anger bubbling in the pit of her stomach. It was a struggle to hold herself back.

"He whines about being insufficiently provisioned in Gascony. When we refuse him and tell him to manage things on his own income, which should be more than enough to do something as simple as keep Gascony secure, he goes behind his father's back and tries to make deals with King Louis." She smiled. "Did you think he would not tell us? Why do you think this treaty was pushed through so quickly? The two of you are still children. Petulant children that need to be taught a lesson."

Eleanor hid her hands beneath the table for they were clenched into tight fists. It took all her years of training to remain seated, but she couldn't bring herself to reply. So Queen Alienor was content to paint them as villains. She could tell it was no use arguing with her over the semantics.

"Prince Edward is a loyal son who works endlessly for this kingdom. He has ruled Gascony well," Eleanor said at last as the silence stretched on.

Queen Alienor scoffed but turned her attention to the food before her. "At the very least, we've reminded him where his loyalty lies. He can still be taught how to behave."

Eleanor gazed at her husband, who appeared to be having a much better time speaking to his father. He never failed to nod in passing to any noble who caught his eye. He was far more diplomatic than Peter of Savoy, who was busy strutting around the great hall.

After the meal the tables were cleared away to make room for dancing, and Edward led her on to the dance floor.

"Smile, my love, for you look sickly," he murmured in her ear, and she did her best to comply.

They didn't dare speak of anything but pleasantries while they were surrounded by those who were eager to eavesdrop. Even as he twirled her around, they merely smiled at each other and stuck to commenting on the food, the decorations and the new tapestries hanging from the rafters.

Only when they retired for the evening to the cramped apartments they were allotted and pulled the curtains shut on their four-poster bed did they whisper to each other.

"Has your father said anything regarding the Lusignans? Will Joan's lands be restored to her?"

Edward shrugged. "It is his dearest wish to bring them back into the fold, but he doesn't see how it is possible."

"Is it your mother's doing?"

"As much as the council's. Simon doesn't quite trust them not to overstep the mark."

Eleanor bit back a groan of frustration. "One step forward, two back. That always seems to be the way with your parents. Your mother blames us for the hasty treaty they made with France. As though it wasn't them who jumped headlong into signing it." She shook her head. "The French King is certainly enjoying playing with us as though we were his marionettes. He's the one who told your parents that you wrote to him."

"They would've found out regardless. I am at once

powerful and powerless. I am not surprised King Louis would do such a thing. To cause strife in England is to weaken and divide us. I would do the same in his shoes. If only things were different. But come, let us talk of pleasanter things."

"When shall we leave this den of wolves?"

Edward pulled her close. "I do not know. We must prepare ourselves to endure a longer visit. Now that we are here, I don't think we'll be allowed to leave anytime soon."

"Oh Edward, that is terrible."

"It's better this way. I need to let my father see that he can trust me. Perhaps I can convince him that we can work together. He has to see that I only mean to do what is best for England."

Eleanor kept her doubts to herself. That night she dreamed Gascony was set aflame, and she woke up screaming.

While Eleanor joined the Queen's ladies and spent the day with them sewing, taking tours of the gardens or in prayer, Edward joined his father in the council chambers.

Simon de Montfort was there too, but not once did he betray their secret understanding.

It said something about Simon's character that he didn't jump at the chance to cause further strife within the royal family the first chance he got. Or who knows perhaps, Edward bribed him.

Eleanor felt she was inadvertently being kept in the

dark. Edward was often with his father and the other men of the court. He rarely had the chance to speak to her without the risk of being overheard. Left in the dark, she grew restless, certain that trouble was brewing.

A week turned into two, and soon Eleanor grew accustomed to the comings and goings of court life. But she felt her every move was being watched and analyzed. Among the Queen's ladies she was an outcast, kept at arm's length yet never allowed to leave. Joan and the Lusignans had returned to France, though they were no longer banished.

The King and Queen were amassing strength while ensuring any opposition was put down. Loyal adherents were arriving at the castle daily. Most were the Queen's relatives who had been so richly rewarded in the past.

Peter of Savoy was given every honor and walked in front of Prince Edward when going into the great hall for dinner. It was a sign to all that while Edward might be the heir to the throne, he had no power of his own. It was a dressing down that Edward bore with patience, hoping that by biding his time and showing his obedience, he would regain his parents' trust.

In June, the royal faction cast their net and ensnared them all. On his way to a meeting in Parliament, Hugh le Despenser was arrested. Caught unprepared and unarmed, Hugh had no choice but to surrender himself. An ally of Simon de Montfort, this act sent a clear warning to everyone who associated themselves with Simon. King

Henry, pleased with himself and assured of the support of his allies, called for him to be tried for treason.

Edward, unsure what to do, paced around like a caged lion.

"If you stand up now, your father will have every excuse to have you arrested too," Eleanor said, trying to appeal to his rationale.

"This was all a trap. He merely wanted to ensure that I was in no position to protest any of his decisions. We are prisoners in all but name."

Frustrated and unable to fathom how they would get out of this, Eleanor found herself laughing. "Well, I will say this," she said, motioning with her hand to the room. "For a prison this is quite luxurious. Do you think our jailors will complain if we sleep in?" she asked, falling into his arms.

"I don't suppose they will," Edward said, the corners of his lips twitching as he fought back a smile.

She buried her face in his chest, feeling the soft velvet of his coat against her skin. "We'll find a way to escape. This is just the beginning. They want to have Simon de Montfort hanged as a traitor."

Edward was silent as he thought. "Would it be the worst thing if we let nature take its course? We don't owe Simon any loyalty."

Pulling away she looked into his face. "Edward, we made a pact with him."

Edward was unmoved and it didn't sit right with her. It became imperative to convince him. She knew that reality couldn't be like a fairy story, but she needed him to be the chivalrous knight of her imagination.

"It's not only that — he's the only one who has

supported you, and he kept his promises to provide you with men and money to hold Gascony. More and more you agree with his policies. I believe if he disappears this would only strengthen your parents' position. Who would speak out against their excesses then?"

Edward let out a deep breath. "I see your point, but I dare not openly declare myself as his friend. My parents wouldn't hesitate to charge me as well."

Eleanor nodded. "Certainly. We shall have to think about it. If there's a trial, surely the jury could be swayed. Or at the very least, bribed."

He chuckled. "And there I was thinking you were incorruptible. Turns out my wife is just as cunning as I am."

"It's not the same thing and you know it," she huffed, striding over to the bed and sitting on the edge. "Now," she said, smiling coyly. "Let's see if we can't find some way to while away the time in our prison."

"I'm at your command, My Lady."

Two days later the Queen rode to New Forest to hunt deer. Grateful for the change of scenery, Eleanor leaped at the chance to go with her. It was unusual for the women of the court to ride out, but they were heavily guarded by men at arms and had huntsmen to help flush out their quarry.

This strange party of hunters was a small sampling of most of the factions at court. It included Lady Margaret de Quincy, Countess of Lincoln, and Lady Joan de Stuteville, wife to Hugh Bigod, the former Justiciar of England, and it certainly made for a competitive outing.

There was jostling for who would go first, who would take the first shot, and boasting was the primary form of communication among the ladies. Eleanor, following closely behind on Queen Alienor's mount, kept to herself.

"You were quite eager to ride out with us," Queen Alienor said, craning her head to look at her. "Now you are as quiet as a mouse."

Lady Margaret hid a laugh behind a cough.

"Being here in the forest takes my breath away. I am honored merely to be in your presence, Your Grace," Eleanor said, glancing around the thicket they had ridden into.

In the distance, they could hear the baying of hunting dogs. They'd picked up the scent. Queen Alienor's horse pulled against his reins, eager to give chase, but the Queen held him back.

"The New Forest is a beautiful but haunted place. Do you know its history?" she asked.

Eleanor sensed a trap but was unable to see how to side-step the question. "Yes. It is where the tragic death of King William Rufus, son of William the Conqueror, took place. May they both rest in peace."

Queen Alienor grinned. "Indeed. Many say it was a stray arrow that led to his death, but I speculate it was foul play. He was unpopular." She patted her horse's neck with a gloved hand.

The other ladies glanced at each other, feeling uncertain about what she could mean by this comment.

"Here is something you won't read in that library of yours. King William was too careless with his safety. He allowed those ambitious family members of his free rein, and he paid for it. We must learn from our forefathers, must we not?"

Eleanor felt her stomach churn.

Queen Alienor gave a shake of her head as though she were greatly distressed by the thought. "I, for one, shall never make the mistake of trusting anyone fully. Vipers are everywhere."

So she knew, or at least suspected, that for all Edward's kowtowing to his parents and playing the part of the obedient son, he was merely waiting for his chance. Eleanor had seen this game played before, and if Queen Alienor was hoping to scare her into making a confession, she would be disappointed.

"Your Grace, I believe they have found a stag." Her ears had picked up the call of the hunters. She didn't urge her horse on but waited patiently for the Queen to take action.

All the Queen's good humor had melted away and a scowl replaced the complacent smile. Before she could say anything else, her man at arms appeared in the thicket, his eyes wide with anticipation.

"Hurry, Your Grace. We've cornered the beast."

Having no choice, Queen Alienor, spun round and urged her horse through the forest. It was she who used a crossbow to deal the killing blow to the tired creature.

The delay had resulted in the deaths of two of the hunting dogs, who were speared by the antlers of the furious stag. Eleanor couldn't help but feel sorry for both the dogs and the stag. Any enjoyment of the day had vanished in that thicket, and it all felt like a waste.

The victorious huntresses returned to the castle. The

King commended his wife and in an unusually jolly mood kissed her full on the lips in front of the gathered court.

Eleanor's eyes met Edward's, and she saw her own concern reflected back to her.

Later that night, as the celebrations raged on and Edward's parents gambled with wild abandon, they retreated to their private chamber and held each other.

"We must take care. I fear we are in danger," Edward said, but he didn't name the threat.

Four days later, as Simon de Montfort was boarding a barge on the River Thames, he was apprehended by the King's men. He was arrested for treason and was to be brought to trial for his crimes against the kingdom.

When Edward heard the news, he overturned the table he'd been writing at. Eleanor rushed to his side to try to placate him.

"Husband, be at peace."

His eyes were wild with rage, but he didn't push her away or reprimand her.

"I am sure justice will be done," she said, being purposefully obtuse. Servants were in and out of their room carrying away dirty linen, while others scoured the fireplace. Now they rushed forward to clean up the food and papers Edward had sent flying.

His hand covered hers, and he took a steadying breath before releasing it. "I apologize. The news was shocking. I am tired of the kingdom being so divided. We should be fighting the heretics in the Holy Land, or the French — not each other."

Eleanor leaned against him, wanting nothing more than the comfort of his embrace. "We can weather any storm."

"Together." He pressed his forehead against hers. After a moment's contemplation he pulled away. "There's something I need to do. Take care of yourself."

She frowned at him but dared not inquire further about what he was planning. "Do you need me to—"

"Rest. Enjoy yourself. Spend the day however you like. I shall return before night falls."

Clutching her hands together, she nodded and curtseyed to him. With a quick kiss on the cheek he was gone. Off to stir up trouble, no doubt. She watched him go with a faint smile on her lips, as though she was some fool who didn't know better.

With nothing to do, Eleanor went to the Queen's apartments, hoping to glean some new information.

The Queen's presence chamber was packed with people, many of them seeking her patronage. They slid away from Eleanor as she made her way through the crowd. At least she could still command respect.

"Ah, my daughter-in-law has decided to grace us with her company," Queen Alienor said with a laugh. In one hand she held a letter, in the other a goblet filled with red Burgundian wine that sloshed dangerously.

Eleanor bowed low, as was expected, and took an empty seat among the Queen's ladies. The mood was celebratory. The royalists were in the ascendency. They felt that with Lord Simon's arrest, they had recaptured power over Parliament.

As no one had formally informed her of the arrest, Eleanor didn't comment, but she felt it was foolish for the royalists to celebrate the victory so prematurely. All she hoped for now was that Edward's name wouldn't be dragged into these proceedings. Would the King and Queen disinherit their son if they discovered he had allied himself with Simon? Eleanor was sure they suspected, but for now they had no proof.

Lady Margaret de Quincy regarded her coolly. "What a pretty gown you're wearing."

"Thank you," Eleanor said, smoothing out the skirt. It was of heavy wool, dyed a brilliant crimson and painted along the hem with little castles in a pretty yellow that mimicked gold.

"France has the very best of fashion," Lady Margaret said with a wistful sigh. "But I'm afraid such a flashy gown doesn't suit your complexion. You should really consult with me when you next select a gown."

Eleanor gritted her teeth. It was telling that Lady Margaret felt safe enough to insult her. Her own gown was a gaudy baby blue hemmed with fur. With her fair complexion and hair, it made her appear sallow and sickly. There was no use arguing with her, but she kept in mind that the woman was no friend.

The Queen called for musicians, and they all settled down to listen to them play a lively song. The day took a festive turn and the entertainment went on well into the night. Eleanor continued to be the butt of the Queen's and her ladies' jokes, but she bore it all with dignity. She was of the enemy — at least, that was how she was made to feel. Was it wise to treat her thus, when one day the tables could turn? Thinking of that day, Eleanor tempered her reactions with a passive smile.

After failing to goad her into reacting, they focused on celebrating and even joked about how they might divide up the Earl of Leicester's properties amongst themselves. Eleanor wondered what the men would say if they could hear the women now. They were certainly a far cry from the innocent fair maidens that appeared in popular ballads.

The days dragged on and the great men of the realm, including Simon's adherents, made their way to the capital for the trial. As preparations began in earnest, so did the backroom dealings. Secret letters were exchanged and meetings were held in shadowed alcoves. Bargains were struck and bets were laid on the outcome of the trial. It was the royal party against the barons. No one could guess who would emerge victorious in this silent battle of wills.

Eleanor wished she could attend the first day of the trial, but women were forbidden from the courtroom.

"I deserve to be there as much as you," she said to Edward, exasperated at being left out.

Her husband kissed her brow. "If I could, I would have you at my side. You know that, but there is nothing I can do about it. Besides, it would be unseemly."

She frowned at him. "What could be so shocking to my sensibilities at a trial? Shall it evolve into mortal combat?"

"I wouldn't be surprised," Edward said.

"I don't appreciate your jokes," she said, but then stopped. "Why are you in such good humor?"

"I have it on good authority that all will be well for us and the kingdom."

She stared into those clear blue eyes of his and saw the intensity behind them. "You know something."

He grinned and stepped away from her. "Something you shall hear of in time. I can't take the credit for it, but I'll bet you a gold sovereign that the trial will fail."

"I don't believe I wish to take that bet." Eleanor shook her head in frustration. "You used to tell me everything. Why are you so quiet now?"

"It's not that I don't trust you," Edward said, searching the papers on his desk in a hurry. "But I cannot predict the way this will turn out and I don't wish to give you false hope. And should the worst come to pass then I want you innocent of all dealings."

"Do you think I haven't already been dragged into this?" Eleanor touched his sleeve. "Edward, your mother barely tolerates me. Even if I know nothing and am completely innocent, she won't care. She will find a way to blame me and get rid of me."

"Good thing you are a royal Princess of Castile. The worst that could happen is that you'd return to your beloved land. Think of your brother's worldly court. Would it really be so terrible if you were to go back?"

He was joking, but he couldn't know how deeply his words hurt. Eleanor's heart was hammering in her ears. The only reason she would be sent back to Castile was if Edward died or if their marriage was dissolved.

"What danger has befallen us this time?"

He shook his head. Stubborn to the last, he gave her a

parting kiss. "We shall speak soon. Place your trust in me. All will be well."

"Edward," she shouted after him in a truly unladylike fashion. "You cannot speak so cryptically and then try to assure me nothing is wrong!"

He was halfway out the door and only stopped to blow her a kiss.

She let out a curse under her breath and settled in with her ladies to work on some needlework.

CHAPTER 8

1262-1263, ENGLAND

On the second day of the trial, a royal messenger from Wales arrived bearing terrible news.

"Prince Llywelyn has invaded Builth. We need help immediately."

The great hall erupted into chaos. King Henry attempted to bring order, reminding the lords assembled there of the important ongoing trial, but no one could think about Simon de Montfort when English lands in Wales were being threatened.

"What will you do, Your Grace?" asked the Earl of Norfolk.

"We shall send men. It is nothing but an uprising. Wales certainly has enough of those every season."

Roger Mortimer stepped forward. "This is more serious than that," said the powerful marcher lord. "I've warned you about the Prince, Your Grace. He's gathered the Welsh lords together and even has Irish fighters among his ranks.

It's not only the force he's gathered that concerns me but the loyalty he has sparked in the common people. Rumors have spread even into England that he is King Arthur reborn. With every victory my men begin to believe that it is true and grow fearful. Indeed, Prince Llywelyn flies the dragon as his standard."

"Cowards," laughed the Earl of Norfolk.

"What did you say?" Lord Roger said, his hand flying to the empty scabbard at his belt.

Surrounded by friends and in full view of the King, the Earl of Norfolk felt confident enough to continue harassing the marcher lord. "I believe you heard me the first time, My Lord. But if your hearing is failing you in your old age then let me repeat myself. Your men are cowards."

Angry shouts erupted around the room.

At Eleanor's side, Edward gripped the silver fork in his hand tightly.

"Leave, Eleanor," he whispered to her. "It won't be safe if things continue like this."

Eleanor shook her head, eyes wide. "I won't leave your side."

"This is not a joke. My father has no control over his own lords. I command you to leave."

The marcher lord was face to face with the Earl of Norfolk. They might not have weapons on hand, but they were moments away from coming to blows, like brawlers in the street. Men were crowding around them; insults and angry words were being thrown around on both sides.

Eleanor didn't move. "You must stop this, Edward."

He glanced at his father, who was waving helplessly at the lords. He hadn't even called for his guards.

Perhaps it was Eleanor's determination to remain by his side that made Edward spring into action. He stood and bellowed loudly, "My lords, what madness is this that sets us at each other's throats when England is besieged by enemies? On behalf of my father, I, Edward, Prince of England, command you to return to your seats."

His words echoed around the room, and the raw emotion in his voice seemed to penetrate even the most addled mind. They all froze and turned as one to regard him on the dais.

In this moment, Edward, already towering over most men, with burning fury in his eyes, was intimidating.

"It is an outrage to see the lords of this realm behave like wild savages, and in the King's castle too."

They bowed their heads, allowing a man nearly half the age of most to castigate them. One by one they dropped to their knees and begged King Henry for forgiveness.

Stunned, he accepted their apologies and bid them rise. For a moment the King just stared at them, but at Edward's prompting, said, "My lords, we shall retire to discuss this news in council. Let us leave the ladies to finish their meal in peace."

There was a murmur of agreement as they all had the sense to remember their manners and good sense.

Edward hung back as his father went forward to lead the way to his private council chambers.

"You should've fled," he said to Eleanor in gentle reproach. "This could've turned ugly."

"I am not afraid of anything but being apart from you," she whispered just as fiercely.

He leaned down and claimed her lips with his own. "I shall keep that in mind, my love."

"You will tell me everything that is said, won't you?" she asked, seeing how eager he was to follow the others.

He smiled. "I would bring you with me if I could."

She watched him go, full of apprehension even as she trusted him to look after himself.

The noble ladies of England were still gathering themselves as he left, and Eleanor, not wishing to be around or face the Queen's ire, fled back to her apartments.

A few hours later, Edward found her pulling threads out of a piece of poorly done embroidery.

"You are vicious with that pair of scissors. I would send you into battle if I could. All our enemies would flee before you."

She nipped the thread. "As well you should. I can certainly keep a cool head better than some men. But if you seek to mock me then be warned — I am armed," she said, waving the scissors in his direction.

He held up his hands in mock surrender.

"Is there to be war?" she asked, but his good humor told her that the news from the council was good.

"Simon de Montfort has been called upon to lead a force into Wales and defeat the self-proclaimed ruler of Wales."

Eleanor leaped to her feet, her needlework falling to the floor. "What?"

"And I am to go with him," Edward added, an edge of pride clear in his voice.

"So he is to go free? Are the charges to be dropped?"

Edward nodded. "Simon de Montfort is too valuable,

and my father doesn't have another commander that he can offer in exchange. At least, not one that the others would listen to. I am honored by the chance to prove myself here in England."

"It should go a long way to dispel the rumors you are a spoiled prince."

He grinned. "There are many times when I wish I was exactly that. It would be so much easier to sit back in some castle, taxing my vassals and enjoying the comforts of a warm fire and my doting wife."

She threw a kerchief at him. "What wife wants such a lazy dolt of a husband? I am happy that matters have been settled so neatly, though I wish you didn't have to go into battle. I don't suppose I could accompany you?"

"Out of the question. But I shall be sure to hurry back to you. Robert Leyburn writes to me that the Viscount of Béarn is stirring up trouble in Gascony. I wouldn't be surprised if soon we will be sailing back across the channel to help defend against another invasion."

"Our life is certainly not dull."

Eleanor sat by the window, her head cocked, listening for the sound of trumpets that would announce the return of Edward and Simon de Montfort.

Heralds had already forewarned the castle of their approach. They were victorious in chasing off the Welsh rebels and recapturing the English lands. Eleanor was glad of the victory but abhorred war. Most of the land was set aflame and the populace chased out of their homes. The region would face a hard winter as they regrouped and tried to salvage what they could. Only peace would see Wales prosper, and she hoped she would live to see that happen.

Now she merely longed to be reunited with her husband. She had news for him, and she wasn't sure how he would react. While he was campaigning and fighting, her body waged its own private assault that saw her sick morning and night. The slightest smell might set her off, and after four weeks, the midwife had confirmed Eleanor was carrying a child.

After so many years, it was a blessing indeed.

The trumpets blared, announcing the army's return. Eleanor got to her feet, her hand drifting to her stomach. Surely his victory and her fertility were an omen of good things to come.

Edward rode with his entourage, sitting proudly on his warhorse. He had the weariness of a soldier who slept on hard ground and hadn't known where his next meal was coming from. But all this was tempered by the heady sense of victory. He had proven his strength and cunning on the field of battle. Indeed, even though he rode behind Simon de Montfort, Eleanor could see that it was Edward many of the men were looking to and cheering.

It was Edward who had emerged as the hero of this excursion. Eleanor knew that if she peered into the minds of the gathered crowd, she would find anticipation for the day they would once again have a warrior king to lead them to victory.

Simon jumped from his horse, bowed to the King and presented him with the banner of the fallen Prince of

Wales. Edward followed suit and they were both greeted by King Henry with warm words of welcome and gratitude.

Eleanor caught Edward's eye and a smile broke through her impassive mask of courtly indifference. She longed to be alone with him, but alas, now they would retire to the great hall where the Queen had commanded a royal feast to celebrate the victories in Wales.

"I am glad to see you again," he murmured to her as they walked arm in arm. Candles burned brightly from the chandelier above them. "But is it my imagination or are you looking pale?" Unable to help himself he reached over and touched her cheek.

She leaned into his touch, smiling at his concern. "I'm afraid that is all your doing."

"What do you mean?" he asked. "Were you so worried about me that it drove you to sickness?"

Queen Alienor, who was just a few steps ahead, craned her neck and said, "Your wife is with child. You must congratulate her."

Eleanor's face fell. This wasn't how she'd imagined telling Edward, but when had anything in her life gone as planned?

Edward gripped her hand in his. "Is it true?"

"Yes," Eleanor whispered.

He came to a stop then and kissed her passionately. "Then my victory is complete."

"Shush. Don't tell anyone yet," Eleanor hurried to add. "It's early days. The midwife says..."

"Damn what the midwife says." He laughed and kissed her again. Then realizing the commotion and embarrassment he was causing, he called out his apologies. "We shall discuss this more later when we are alone," he whispered to her.

"I am eager to hear more about your campaign as well."

"And you shall."

"Our Prince was a brave warrior." Simon de Montfort had appeared behind him, clapping him on the back. "He kept his head, in more ways than one."

Those around them laughed at the jest but Edward stiffened. Eleanor wondered if there was something in Simon's tone that displeased him? Or if he'd simply grown to dislike Simon?

The great hall was decorated with the banners of all the nobles who had ridden out to fight, but the biggest, and the one given prominence, was the King's. Henry sat enthroned on a raised dais, above everyone — including his own son — wearing his crown with the Queen at his side. Even as the bards celebrated the victory and the bravery of the English knights, the majority of the praise was heaped onto the King.

It wasn't lost on anyone that he had neither led the army himself, nor planned out the battle strategy. While his lords applauded politely, only the Queen was earnest in her praise.

That night, as Edward brought spiced wine and sweetmeats to their bedroom, they sat in the glowing warmth of the fire and he told her everything.

"De Montfort is a good commander. He plans for every eventuality. I have much to learn from him," Edward said, though it sounded like it was a hard thing for him to admit.

"You've allied yourself with the right people. You should be proud you can identify your own weaknesses, even if you do so begrudgingly. There will always be someone smarter or stronger than you." Eleanor leaned into him. "Overconfidence has been the death of many men."

"Has it?"

She looked up at him. "Shall I give you a history lesson, My Lord? I have a book here somewhere I could read to you from."

He ran his hands through her loose hair. "That would bring me much comfort."

She raised an eyebrow. "I thought you would laugh at the very notion. There are other things we could be doing."

He laughed at her innuendo. "My love, I must take care with you now. You are carrying our child and maybe even the future heir of this realm. I dare not risk either of you."

She pulled away from him so they were eye to eye. "I'm not so delicate as that. Or is it that you've grown bored with me? Perhaps you found yourself a mistress while you were away on campaign. I know that is the way with men. I wouldn't blame you, but I would have you be honest with me."

His eyes widened and then he let out a loud booming laugh. "I don't need a mistress. You keep me busy enough," he teased, then his face grew serious. "I swear I've never been unfaithful to you, and I never will."

She swatted him on the shoulder gently. "You don't need to make such promises to me. It is hard for men and the temptation can grow strong." She sniffed, already knowing it would hurt her, nonetheless. "I don't care as long as I am the only one you love and cherish."

He held her hand and pulled her close. "You ought to have a better opinion of me. You'd think after all these years you'd trust me. I don't say those words lightly. My heart beats for you. I need no other."

She lost herself in the blue depths of his eyes. In a world full of treachery and deceit, she allowed herself this one luxury — she would trust her husband.

———

As the heat of summer settled upon England, Edward's popularity among the barons and England's other magnates was in the ascendency.

After the campaign in Wales, he no longer held back on being outspoken against his father's policies. Before, no one would've paid attention to him, or his parents would silenced him, but with Simon de Montfort's support he had a say.

Eleanor was proud of him. She only wished she had been able to do her part to make his rise to prominence complete. Not a week after Edward's return from Wales, she lost the baby. It was early days, and she was reassured it was common, but it felt like a door shut in her heart forever.

Children left this world too easily. Even those who had yet to be born.

Edward had been attentive and was more concerned about the melancholy that had descended upon her.

"There will be others," he assured her. "And if there's not, I have nieces and nephews enough to adopt as my own."

She forced herself to nod and smile. "I am just lost. Perhaps I am competitive with you. As you rise in the world, I feel like I remain stagnant."

"Then let me give you a greater purpose to occupy your time," he said, as they strolled through the gardens at Westminster. The roses were in full bloom this time of year, filling the air with their heady scent. She watched him pull a sheath of parchment from his lapel and hand it to her.

She studied the seal. *Robert Leyburn.* "Has something happened?"

"Read it for yourself." He motioned for her to sit down on a bench, but she remained standing and paced before him while he sat leisurely with his elbows resting on his knees.

The letter began with assurances from Robert that everything was operating smoothly, but someone had set fire to a tenant's farm not far from their castle. They were investigating the matter and hoping this wasn't the start of some incursion by the Duke of Toulouse into Gascony, or some other baron stirring up revolt and rebellion. The letter urged Edward to return, as his presence would do much to settle the growing discontent.

"It is hard to manage a duchy from afar," Eleanor commented as she refolded the letter and handed it to him. "Will you leave England now?"

Edward shook his head. "I'm finally somewhere I can make a real difference. If I leave, then I will lose their support and we will go back to writing letters begging for aid. They would fall on deaf ears while the real struggle happens here."

"So what do you propose? Robert made it sound urgent."

He ran a hand over his jaw. "I have half a mind to send you there in my place. What would you say to that?"

She gasped. "You would trust me to manage this?"

"We are of one mind. I trust you with our affairs. Besides, I can see how unhappy you are at court. My mother isn't the most welcoming of women. We wouldn't be apart for long. If peace is restored quickly then return to me, and if it's not then rest assured I shall hurry to Gascony."

"Very well," Eleanor said, her heart swelling with pride at the thought of him trusting her with so much power. Whether or not she was allowed to hold equal power in the eyes of the law or council did not matter, for he valued her highly and in the end that was all she could ask for.

As she prepared to return to Gascony, Eleanor was witness to the power struggle between the two factions at court. Edward was quickly gathering his own supporters and was playing the role of mediator between them, even though he often sided with Simon de Montfort these days.

"I will not allow your cousin to hold the Bishopric of Durham," Simon said to the Queen, not bothering to hide his contempt.

She ignored him and turned to the monks who'd journeyed all the way to London to vote on this matter. "God knows the piety of my cousin is famous. He has done good works for Christians and even pledged to contribute to the next crusade."

"Then he ought to go and spare us all this trouble," Edward whispered in Eleanor's ear. She bit her lip to keep a laugh from escaping.

She'd all but demanded to be allowed to sit in on this

meeting. Since Queen Alienor was present there was no reason Eleanor could not be as well.

"The piety of your cousin is not in question, Your Grace," the most senior of the monks said, bowing his tonsured head in reverence to her. "We are merely trying to determine the best candidate for the post."

Queen Alienor's hands clenched into fists. To her the matter was settled. She wished to appoint who she wanted to the post. Simple as that. As Queen it was in her power to award prestigious titles and lands to whoever she pleased. But this was a power that both the King and Queen had abused far too often in the past. They weren't concerned with who would do the best job, merely who would support them in the future.

Wasn't this how they lost so much land in France?

"I hope you will consider Brother Eamond," Simon began. "He has been educated at Oxford and is well versed in canon law—"

He was interrupted by a scoff from the Queen. "A lawyer." She waved her hand dismissively in his direction. "Would you have a mere lawyer as a bishop?"

Edward cleared his throat. "I have a third possibility."

The room fell quiet as all attention turned to him, but the silence merely encouraged him to continue. "Father Andrew of Kent. He has served his congregation for many years, and like Brother Eamond has studied at Oxford. He is a loyal Englishman and the reports I've received of him speak highly of his honest and godly character."

Queen Alienor's lips thinned. She looked ready to scold her son, but held back while the elderly priests of Durham considered the possibility.

"We have heard of him."

To his credit, Simon de Montfort, looked intrigued rather than put out by the prospect of losing the position he had earmarked for one of his own followers.

"We ought to speak to him. It would only be fair. The most important thing is that the right man is found for the post," Simon mused. Then he chuckled. "Shall we adjourn this meeting while we can interview the candidates? I don't suppose Father Andrew is close at hand?"

Edward grinned. "He is passing through London on Pilgrimage."

"How convenient," Queen Alienor said, her voice full of malice. She regarded her son coolly. "I shall excuse myself, then. I hope that you godly men will make the right choice."

They all bowed to her respectfully, but it was clear to everyone that she had lost.

Eleanor wondered if Edward had made the right choice, standing up to his mother so directly. Regardless, it was too late to turn back now. She only hoped that his allies were ready to stand by him.

CHAPTER 9

1263 ENGLAND & GASCONY

Not long after the conference the priests made a decision and elected Edward's choice.

Word spread of how Edward had intervened against the appointment of yet another of his mother's relatives. He'd become something of a hero.

The Queen's heavy campaigning had come to nothing, and she was in a fury. For days after she refused to acknowledge him, while Simon de Montfort tried to claim it as his own victory.

"The man will be impartial and good for our souls," he said, clapping Edward on the back. "The lion cub is finding his roar."

Edward had laughed and invited Simon to go hunting with him on the morrow. "Then you shall see how well I hunt as well."

Simon looked amused.

It was hard for Eleanor to reach Edward's mood when

he was around Simon. But for the moment, the two men had maintained their mutually beneficial alliance.

They balanced each other out. The Earl might have the men, and the support of the barons, but he lacked the proper lineage. Edward's royal blood carried prestige and power. When compared with his parents, he was a voice of reason and restraint. Essentially, he represented a safe middle ground that those who supported royal sovereignty could gather behind.

Perhaps Simon had not foreseen Edward's growing popularity and was still trying to navigate the changing political landscape. But Eleanor couldn't help fearing that he would turn on them.

"You will be careful, won't you?" she said, cupping Edward's face in her hand.

"It is you who should take care," Edward said. "I shall miss you while you are in Gascony."

"Then make sure you hurry back to me," Eleanor said, tears pricking the corners of her eyes.

"I shall write to you as often as I can. Be safe, my love."

They pressed their foreheads together in one last embrace, and then she turned and boarded the ship waiting to carry her across the Channel.

She kept her eyes fixed upon her husband standing on the dock, until he disappeared from view. Even then she didn't turn away, but said a prayer invoking God to watch over him.

In Gascony, she was reunited with Joan who embraced her as though they hadn't seen each other in years.

"It has been lonely without you," she said, as they ascended the steps into the keep. "I made sure the servants cleared out your rooms and laid out fresh rush mats in your bedchamber."

"You have made good use of your time here," Eleanor said.

"Well, with William gone half the time I have little to do," Joan said with a sigh. "At least I have Aymer to keep me on my toes. You wouldn't believe the trouble that boy causes me..." Joan paused, looking at her awkwardly. News of her miscarriage had traveled far. "Anyway, I shouldn't complain."

"You needn't worry about my feelings. There will be others. I have faith and am still young," Eleanor said, surprised to find she was telling the truth. Perhaps it was easier to ignore the pain of the loss when the world around her felt so dangerous. They were on the edge of disaster, and one tragedy couldn't distract her from that.

Joan patted her shoulder. "You are a good friend to me. I am grateful he's a healthy, lively boy. My only hope is that his father will be able to spend more time with him."

"Soon everything will settle down, I promise. Edward is making headway in England, which is why he sent me here," Eleanor said, as they reached her rooms.

Inside, the smell of fresh herbs and clean linen sheets filled the air. She took a seat at her desk, smoothing a hand over the polished surface. "What can you tell me of Gascony?"

Joan looked stunned by the question. "What do you mean?"

"Who is making trouble? Is it my husband's absence that has led to this fresh set of troubles?"

There was a slight tremble in Joan's hand, but she gathered herself. "Perhaps, but there are always those who are unhappy about the state of affairs. Toulouse has been sending arms and coin to the French Viscounts, promising to bring an army if they rise in rebellion."

Eleanor tapped her nails on the wood surface, thinking this over. "King Louis must have given his blessing, otherwise there is no way the Count of Toulouse would dare promise such a thing."

"Lord Guy wishes to attack Toulouse to make a show of strength."

Eleanor inhaled sharply. That is the worst thing they could do, but calmly she asked Joan what her husband thought.

"William wishes to be more cautious. He also fears that if we were to take our men and march into Toulouse, we'd be leaving Gascony undefended. Not to mention that it might give the rebels within our borders a chance to cause some actual harm."

Eleanor pinched the bridge of her nose and sat back in her seat sighing. What was the right answer? Should she be daring or cautious?

"I will rest now, and then I would like to speak to your husband as soon as he is back with the patrol."

"Very well," Joan said, but she hesitated in the doorway. "Is there any news? About my lands, I mean." There was something sheepish, yet hopeful about the way she asked the question. Eleanor wished she didn't have to disappoint her, but her silence was telling all the same.

"Well, I suppose it will take time," Joan said, wringing her hands. "I get so impatient. I apologize."

"I promise one day you will be restored to your proper place."

Joan nodded, but Eleanor caught the glassy look in her eyes and knew she was moments away from crying.

The Lusignans had been loyal to herself and Edward. It wasn't fair they were being punished. Seeing that words would have little effect, she made a promise to herself that she would help see Joan restored to her title. She was a Countess by birth, and her family deserved the security that ought to provide. Besides, William had proven himself as a good commander; he was loyal and just, exactly the sort of man she would wish ruling the Pembroke estates. He would be a good vassal lord they could rely on once Edward took the throne. Eleanor knew it was unchristian of her to hope that he would ascend to his throne sooner rather than later, but the Queen's jealousy shouldn't be allowed to poison the kingdom further.

She shuddered to think how much Queen Alienor had already cost England?

Lord William came to her presence chamber as soon as he arrived in the castle. He paid her all the respect she was due, and after a few banal inquiries as to the state of her health and the welfare of the King and Queen, they quickly moved on to discussing business.

"We received Sir Robert's report that the Viscount of Béarn was stirring up trouble. Can you confirm this? And are we sure it is him?"

"There can be no doubt," William said. "My men

captured two spies in the village. They carried letters bearing his seal."

"That would incriminate them. Assuming they were genuine."

William's eyes widened. "My Lady, I would never make such a grave mistake."

"No, but seals can be stolen and replicated. Are these men still — alive?" She felt awkward asking the indelicate question, but had no other choice.

"They are in the dungeon below. We were planning to ransom them."

"I have a better plan," Eleanor said. "Let us invite the Viscount of Béarn to the castle. His response will tell us all we need to know."

William was taken aback. Even Sir Jasper, who'd been listening, got to his feet. "My Lady, I must counsel you against inviting an enemy amongst us."

"If he comes and swears fealty to me on behalf of my husband, then we will know he's not the cause of this unrest. But he may come storming in with an armed force. We will be prepared either way, and we shall know what to think if he makes excuses about why he cannot come."

Eleanor could sense they were uneasy with her plan, but she'd been considering this on the long journey from England. If he was their enemy, then one way or another they would have to face him. It was better they tried to dictate the terms.

Gaston de Montcada, Viscount of Béarn, traveled through Gascony with a letter of safe conduct signed and sealed by Eleanor. He came with a small number of attendants and was guarded by about twenty men at arms. Hardly an invasion force. Spies along the way kept an eye on everything he did and said. Nothing drew anyone's suspicions. So either he was innocent or he was an adept con man.

Dressed in a regal gown of forest-green silk, Eleanor greeted him in the presence chamber. She had seated herself to the right of the empty ducal throne Edward would have occupied, as a clear reminder that he was in charge and she was only representing him. It gave her greater authority to remind the Count that England, not merely her own County of Ponthieu, was at her back.

"Greetings, Princess," he said in French as he kneeled before the dais. For a proud man this must have been a hard thing to do.

Eleanor regarded his bowed head. Yet, even like this he was not humbled. The straightness of his back and the strength of his carriage marked him as a warrior. There were other signs as well. His face and hands bore the scars of a man who had faced many battles but come out victorious.

Over ten years ago, he had led an army into Gascony. The campaign would have been victorious had the English not snatched away his victory by allying themselves with her family. It was how her marriage came to be.

She ought to thank him for bringing her and Edward together.

"Rise, My Lord," she said. "Thank you for traveling all this way to speak with me."

"I go where I am summoned." He got to his feet in one fluid motion. He gazed at the assembled men and women who were watching. Was he searching for enemies? He looked like a man resigned to his fate.

"You have not always been a loyal vassal in the past," Eleanor said.

"I never claimed to be a perfect man," Lord Gaston said, clasping his hands behind his back. There was no defiance in his expression, only perfect deference to her authority. Yet for all that, he was a proud, unbending man.

"Men have been arrested in the village. They were trying to incite the locals to rise up and storm the castle. When they were searched, we found letters bearing your seal."

The Viscount looked shocked, but he didn't rush to defend himself.

"Was this your doing?"

His eyebrow arched as he glanced around the room. "I didn't know I was to be put on trial. Does it matter what I say?"

Eleanor smiled. "I would like to hear your version of events. My husband wishes for justice to be done."

"It would be a convenient excuse to have me, your one-time enemy, arrested."

"It would," Eleanor said, leaning forward. Nothing about his actions or words indicated a guilty conscience. "But I fear I would be putting an innocent man behind bars while my true enemies remain free."

He studied her carefully, then with a shrug said, "I have not sent men to stir up trouble in your lands. I know it would take more than a rabble of peasants to take this castle and rid Gascony of the English."

She smiled. "At least you are honest, sir. And for a French man that is unusual."

His impassive expression melted away as he grinned. "It is not often I trade insults with women."

"Let us say, I am inclined to believe you. Who do you believe could be behind these insurrections?"

"My Lady, I could not say."

"Try."

"There are many who lay a claim to Gascony. Any one of them could be trying to capture it."

"Especially now that its lord is gone?"

He held up his arms. "I would not venture to guess their thoughts, but trouble in your realm is a benefit to them one way or another."

"You see us as weak."

There was an eruption of displeasure and outrage at her words, but she motioned for silence. Count Gaston's eyes sparked with amusement.

"I would not say that, My Lady. But your king is occupied with other matters. He has given up his claim to many of the French lands, and if there was a time to reclaim those that remain, then it might be now. I, for one, am growing old and have no interest in pursuing such a course of action. The fight between our people goes far back. At one time your parents allied themselves with me, but now enemies," he said, a gentle smile on his features. "It is the way of the world. Perhaps, it is our curse."

"Thank you for your honesty," Eleanor said, then she

looked at Robert Leyburn. "We have room for the Viscount and his men, do we not?"

"Yes, My Lady," Robert said, uncertainly.

"Good." She turned back to Lord Gaston. "You have my thanks for traveling all the way here. If you swear to me now on the Holy Bible that you are not planning some treachery or rebellion, you are free to return to your lands. I hope you will stay a few days to rest and recover. Then you will be able to enjoy some English hospitality."

He bowed at the waist. "I will swear, and may I say, you are as just as you are beautiful, My Lady."

She inclined her head and dismissed him.

Once he was gone, all her advisors and Guy Lusignan leaped to offer their opinions.

"You cannot believe him, My Lady."

"Of course, the Frenchman would lie. Do not let yourself be deceived."

She waved them off and looked at William. "And what do you think?"

"In the past I might have been quick to urge you to detain him as well. But in this case I doubt he is the perpetrator. We ought to focus our attention on fishing out who our real enemy is."

Eleanor nodded. There was a murmur of agreement and Eleanor thanked her lucky stars she had his support in this.

"Very well. Then we have our work cut out for us. Prince Edward will not thank any of us if he returns to chaos and insurrection in his duchy."

With the help of the steward and marshal, Eleanor ordered the countryside scoured for spies and anyone suspected of causing trouble. She sold some of her jewels and they hired mercenaries to help patrol Gascony's borders.

As it turned out, the threat of invasion dissipated as it became clear that this would not be an easy victory.

She felt assured that she had done her duty well.

As promised, Edward's letters arrived with regularity. They could not replace him, but provided a succor for her loneliness.

Then shocking news reached her. King Henry officially repudiated the Provisions of Oxford. He had gone behind Parliament's back and written to the Pope, who then absolved him of any oaths he had made under what the Pope called duress.

The royalist party was making their move to take back power in England.

Eleanor set Edward's coded letter to flame.

As she watched it turn to blackened ashes, she wished their problems could disappear just as quickly.

England had been so close to peace. Now that future was snatched away.

Simon de Montfort left London and many disgruntled nobles were gathering to his side. Civil war was coming.

One day, without warning, her husband appeared on the doorstep.

Eleanor rushed to the courtyard just as Edward was giving instructions to his groom.

"Edward!"

He turned towards the sound of her voice, but although he smiled upon seeing her, there was an emptiness in his eyes that made her stop in her tracks.

"What has happened?"

He took hold of her and they embraced. "My love," he whispered into her hair. "I cannot even begin to tell you of the betrayal I have faced in England."

"Edward. You scare me. What has happened?"

He took a deep breath and pulled her through the doors of the keep. Only in his private chambers did he come to a stop.

"Even now I cannot wrap my head around it. We are ruined."

"Is it Simon?"

Edward let out a laugh. "Hardly. If I had been smarter, I would've thrown my lot in with him."

"Can he not help you, then?"

Edward shook his head. "I'm afraid he's cast me off. I knew our friendship was tentative at best, but I had hoped he would prove to be more faithful than this. Without lands and vassals of my own, I am a worthless worm."

Eleanor arched a brow, but she could see his panic and anger was genuine. "Will you tell me what has happened?"

"My own parents have plotted against me. You were right. My mother is vindictive. This whole time she's been keeping her grievances against me to herself. Now that my father has the support of the Pope, she feels safe to act against me."

Fear tightened its grip on Eleanor and she faltered, feeling dizzy as she imagined he had been disinherited.

"She's taken everything away from me. My lands and titles. I was called before a council which she preceded over. First, she accused Sir Robert of stealing funds from my treasury. It did not matter what evidence I provided to the contrary. In the end, they declared me unfit to rule my lands. My own mother forced me to relinquish ownership of everything in exchange for an allowance. I am a beggar prince."

Eleanor laughed. She couldn't help it. This all felt like a terrible dream.

"I'm glad you find this amusing. I've been gelded. Any ambitions I might have had are gone now."

"You don't understand Edward — I feared far worse."

He kicked at the floorboards. "Oh yes, they threatened to disinherit me. I was trapped in London. If I hadn't agreed to my mother's terms then they would've done it. At least, that's what they claimed. I rue the day I sent you here on your own."

She pushed back the hair from his face so she could look him in the eye. "Never doubt yourself."

He glanced away. "If I had come to Gascony with you, then perhaps none of this would've come to pass. I would've been beyond their reach. But instead, I was forced to bow to their demands. With the Pope and the French King on their side, what could I do?"

Edward wasn't a man to be pitied, but in this moment she felt the need to reach out to him and embrace him.

"My love, you did all you could. Never doubt that. You couldn't have known which way the wind would blow. Who knows what the future will bring?"

"I cannot raise an army; I will be kept impoverished and dependent on my parents."

"Not forever," she said with all the confidence she could muster. "You were a threat to them, and they sought to undermine you. But they cannot change who you are and the fact that one day, you will rule as King of England. Do not let this be your defeat. Look to the future."

He kissed her then. The full force of his emotions was expressed in this one act. The love. The frustration.

They lost themselves in this moment of wild abandon.

Now that Edward was back in Gascony he could finish the work she had begun. Raising what loyal adherents they had with promises of looting, Edward rode out to raid their neighbors to the north and south. It wasn't open war, but the plunder they seized and the disquiet they caused meant that Gascony's own borders were left alone.

With his Lusignan kinsmen at the helm, they pushed back on the French incursion into their land. The farmers returned to their fields, no longer afraid of raiders in the night.

While the situation back in England was uncertain, at least here in Gascony, Edward had proven his worth.

CHAPTER 10

1263, GASCONY & ENGLAND

Edward came bursting into Eleanor's room. "We must go!"

Her maids were startled, and stared wide-eyed as he intruded on this feminine space and began raiding it. He flung open the lids on her chests and rifled through her things.

Eleanor watched as everything of value disappeared into a burlap sack. She scented danger in the air, but her good humor overcame her.

"Have you come to rob me, husband?" Eleanor set aside her needlework and stood.

She'd been sitting before the fire, her hands idle, as the flames licked the air. Troublesome thoughts had threatened to overcome her as she mulled over the events that brought her here. Always on alert. Always ready to flee from one danger or another.

When had she last felt safe?

She thought of her lands in Ponthieu, then her mind flew further back to her homeland in Spain. Only there, under the warm Castilian sun, had she felt secure. Even though she was certain a bright future lay ahead of her, she shivered against the rough sea of her anxieties as they buffeted her, threatening to drag her down into the depths of melancholia. There was only one person she could rely on, and right now he was deaf to her. She could see from his tense shoulders that he was lost in his thoughts, so she straightened and called again.

"Edward."

Finally, he stilled. Blinking away whatever dark thoughts plagued him, he turned to her. Eleanor wanted nothing more than to wrap her arms around his neck and pull him close. Together they could weather any storm. She only wished he could be as assured of that as she was.

"My love, there is no time. We must flee back to England."

She swallowed hard. "What has happened?" They were all but in exile here in Gascony, ever since his parents had stripped him of his lands and independence. Truly, trouble could come from any quarter. There was no use trying to guess from where. The King, the Queen, foreign powers, the powerful English barons — any of these could have caused his distress.

"The Welsh have raised an army and there is more trouble besides that for me to contend with." His lips thinned, in unconcealed rage. Too angry to go on he merely shook his head. "We will go to London. I have friends there who will stand by me."

He was being vague. Eleanor would've liked to ask him

more, but she was acutely aware of the listening ears of her maids. Any one of them could be a spy.

She motioned for them to come forward. "You heard the Prince. Pack up whatever you can. If you aren't ready to leave with the rest of the party, then you will be left behind."

Some skittered away, others stayed and began to rip the linen off her bed and pull the fine gowns off pegs to be folded away in trunks.

"We will need to travel light," Edward said, his tone soft.

She shook her head. Beneath the veil covering her head her dark tresses swung side to side.

"Eleanor, we have no time to lose. I don't wish to argue with you," he whispered, as he took her hands in his and drew her close.

"You've made it clear that trouble is brewing once more. You will need more than just the gold chalices you pilfered from my room. They might buy you temporary favor with a few lords, but it will not be enough."

His blue eyes were hard, but by now he knew far better than to leap into anger. Patiently he waited for her to gather herself. Truth be told, Eleanor hadn't been settled on her course of action either.

"I will not be returning with you to England," she said, leaning forward. "We will go our separate ways. You will go to London while I go to my mother in Ponthieu." Then she added in a low whisper, "Once there I will raise our levies to fight for us. As my mother's heir, I have a right. Once I have an army at my back I will return to you."

"Bless you, wife," Edward said. His expression was full of love and awe.

She fell into a curtesy and looked up at him from beneath her lashes. "It is merely my duty as a wife to serve my husband's needs."

He guffawed and she raised her chin higher so he might see the grin on her face and the coyness in her eyes.

Raising her up he pulled her into his arms and his mouth fell upon hers. The passion of his kiss surprised her at first, but she melted into his touch and snaked her arms around his neck, pressing herself against him. It was shameful for them to be acting like this, especially in front of her attendants, but the taste of indecency was never so sweet. In times like these, such breaches of decorum ought to be excused.

"If only there was more time," he whispered as he pulled away, his hand gripping the back of her gown as though he would rip it from her.

"We won't be apart for long, My Lord," she said.

He grinned. "Would you make a solemn oath to that effect?"

"I would." She pulled him back towards her again, feeling the strength of him against her. Then she released him and bid him a proper farewell. "Godspeed, husband."

"Promise you won't dawdle. There's nothing in this castle worth losing your freedom over."

She listened to his retreating steps and the sound of his voice as he shouted to his men.

Her women looked to her for guidance.

"My husband is right. We won't have time to dawdle while I pack away all my finery." She looked wistfully for a moment at the crimson silk etched with a silver hem. "I will need practical gowns for this journey, and my jewels. We shall have to limit ourselves to what can fit in saddlebags for we will have to travel light and fast. Send for the steward. I wish to speak to him at once."

There was a pause before they began scrambling to do her bidding. Eleanor only hoped that the excitement of this sudden departure would keep them occupied and that no one would have time to send a secret message.

She turned her back to the fire as a maid doused the flames. The logs hissed and crackled their displeasure, sending a cloud of thick smoke around her. She closed her eyes and imagined Queen Alienor's face when she heard of their escape. It would be too late for her to do anything, but she wasn't the sort of woman to take it so easily or forget.

Before mid-afternoon, Eleanor was on the road. Her husband had not specified the threat heading their way — there had been no time — but it wasn't necessary. Their trust in each other was so unshakeable that when one said run, the other ran. No questions asked.

As she rode, she kept looking over her shoulder, her keen eyes looking for the telltale signs of dust being kicked up in the distance by a traveling army. The horizon remained an unbroken picture of peace and tranquility. From this, Eleanor had to assume they were safe.

Glancing around at the men and women accompanying her, she could sense their unease. Even the animals pulled against their reins and pawed at the ground, as though sensing the mounting anxiety in the air.

Eleanor found herself smiling, a habit she had formed in times of strife and unrest. Her faith in God was strong; she felt protected by the knowledge that her fate was in His hands and it comforted her. How could she comfort her people? They looked to her for guidance.

She recalled the works of the famous troubadour Bernart de Ventadorn. Letting inspiration take her where it may, she cleared her throat and began to sing in high Occitan:

"It's no wonder if I sing
Better than any other singer,
For my heart goes more towards love,
And I am more skilled in its service.
Heart and body and wisdom and sense
And strength and power are in me;
Love draws me into its freshness
That in no other way I await..."

At first her escort was stunned, and worried about who might overhear, but slowly others who knew the words took up the tune and added their voices to hers.

"...That I may never live another day or month.
Since I will be despised by it,
And I will no longer have a desire for love."

As the song ended, one of her knights took out a flute and played a Castilian tune she recognized. She tilted her head in his direction.

"This is a song from my brother's court," she announced, in a loud clear voice. "It was sung to celebrate the Virgin Mary while we processed through the streets."

She closed her eyes, tapping her fingers against her knees as she let the light, playful tune carry her away. Confident she remembered the words, she began to sing once more.

"Holy Mary, star of the day,
Show us the way to God and guide us.
For you make those who have gone astray see
That they were lost through sins,
Understanding how very guilty they are;
But through you, they are forgiven
For their audacity..."

The tune, in contrast to the lyrics, was uplifting. Soon everyone was smiling and clapping along as they made their way through the French countryside.

"I thank you, good knight," Eleanor called as the song ended. "You have transported me back to Castile."

"I've often found that music has that power, my lady," the knight replied, bowing his head politely. "Your father was famous for his wisdom and beautiful compositions."

Overcome by curiosity, she ventured to ask, "How is it you know his works so well?"

The knight blushed at being singled out. "My father was an ambassador to your father's court. He was honored upon his return to England with a copy of his works."

"And your father? Does he still live?"

"No, My Lady. He died before I came into your service."

"I wish I could've met him. But I am pleased he shared what he learned with his children."

"It's not hard to see why. Though he was loyal to England and an Englishman through and through, I believe he loved Castile and dreamed of the warm sun every time the winter gales buffeted our castle."

Eleanor's heart swelled. "It is hard to forget a place like Castile. But just as he learned to love it, I have learned to love England and France. If only God in his wisdom had decided to shorten the distance between the kingdoms."

"Shall I play you another?"

"If you please. Though I fear I am too tired to add my voice to your lute."

As they rode on, listening to his gentle music, a sense of peace overcame her.

The further she traveled from the castle, the more she regretted not taking her time to bring along more belongings. Her husband had taken all the gold he could get his hands on. She didn't begrudge him that. He would need it to pay for his passage home and to keep the men loyal to him. Not to mention what Parliament might demand of him. She grimaced at the very thought of their hard-earned treasure disappearing into the hands of greedy barons or mercenaries who would surely seize their chance now that he was at their mercy. She could only hope that they would be too busy uniting against their common enemy to waste time being petty to Edward.

But she was more worried about the small collection of manuscripts she had accumulated over the years than the gold. The knowledge she'd gathered there was more precious to her than anything. Even in such times of darkness.

As they neared the sea, the safer they felt. News began to trickle in and though the sources couldn't always be verified, Eleanor better understood the threat they faced. Both

Simon de Montfort's faction and Queen Alienor were keen on taking control of England. The means by which this could be accomplished was to have both the King and his heir in their keeping.

Queen Alienor, against the wishes of Parliament, had stayed in France with Edward's youngest brother Edmund. The French King had granted them sanctuary and his protection. Other rumors claimed that she had gone to Flanders to raise an army to fight the barons of England. Meanwhile, Simon de Montfort had gathered a large force and was seeking to take possession of key castles throughout English held territories. All the while, he was scouring the countryside looking for the Prince.

War was inevitable now and though Eleanor tried to keep abreast of everything that was happening, but she couldn't be sure of anything.

All Eleanor knew was that she had to hurry with all urgency to her mother in Ponthieu.

Once they reached the coast, they boarded a ship that spirited them up the French coast, careful to avoid the English navy that might seize them. Good winds and fair weather ensured the journey went smoothly. Eleanor remained at the helm throughout, unable to take her eyes off the horizon. She had told no one, not even Edward, but she once again felt the telltale signs of pregnancy. She had missed her courses twice and the smell of food made her nauseous. Even now on the ship, she felt like hurling the contents of her meager breakfast into the sea below, but she fought the impulse, refusing to allow herself to succumb to weakness.

After a week of travel, Abbeville came into view. The

capital city of the province she would one day inherit was a blessed sight indeed.

A formal entourage of guards and heralds greeted them. They led the way to the castle, clearing a path through the busy streets as the citizens gathered to watch and wave.

In the ancient castle steeped in history, her mother, the Countess Joan, ruled alongside her second husband.

Eleanor had never met him, but she had no time to worry about what he thought or if he made her mother happy. Her thoughts were only on Edward, and every moment she wasted was a moment he could be in danger.

Her mother, Lady Joan, greeted her at the castle gates. It was the first time they'd seen each other in more than ten years. After Eleanor's father's death, her mother had not tolerated her stepson's rule. Things came to a head when she was accused of plotting against him. Rather than face a trial or continue to try to live in such a hostile environment, she returned to rule Ponthieu and married a petty lord.

Rarely, if ever, did she write to Eleanor, who often wondered if her mother cared about her.

A knight helped her down from her mount. Eleanor was grateful, as her balance was unsteady after spending all that time at sea.

She approached her mother with her head held high, and curtseyed politely, keeping in mind that as Princess of Castile and wife of the heir to the English Crown, she outranked her.

The Countess exclaimed at the sight of her and curtseyed formally too, before embracing her tightly.

"My daughter, it has been far too long!" Lady Joan said. "You've become such a beauty. Let me look at you." She held her at arm's length, her eyes squinting. "What a Queen you shall make one day."

Eleanor's smile was strained. That future felt so uncertain now.

A man stepped forward from behind her mother, and Eleanor assumed this was her stepfather. He was unassuming but had a courteous countenance that she appreciated.

Her mother took her hand and led her inside. Eleanor studied her as she began to prattle on about family news. She had grown plump since the last time she'd seen her, and the hair peeking out from beneath her veil had turned gray, yet she was still as lively and energetic as Eleanor remembered. Even at her age one could still call her handsome. As they continued walking, Lady Joan spoke of everything and nothing, never giving Eleanor a moment to speak.

"I have arranged for a series of entertainments every day you are here." She stopped to giggle. "Though I suppose I don't know how long you will be staying. In any case, there will be a tournament and then we shall go hunting, there will be a bear baiting and—"

"Lady Mother, thank you, but I did not come here seeking refuge. I came here as your heir to ask for your assistance. There is great unrest in England. I need an army, not acrobats."

Her mother stopped short. "My dear, it is not so simple as that..."

Eleanor blinked, unsure why she was surprised to find nothing in her life could ever be simple.

"What your mother means is, we simply don't have the funds," Lord Jean, her stepfather, explained.

"But you do for entertainments?" Eleanor frowned.

"Well. They are a necessity," said her mother, "and besides, Viscount Francois provided the musicians as a gift. But now let me show you to your chambers. I have prepared everything for you. I am sure you will want to rest. Will you be joining your mother-in-law in Paris?"

Eleanor, still reeling from the reunion with her mother, could only shake her head.

Seeming to understand, her mother patted her hand and said, "Silly me, pushing you like this. You look pale and clammy — you aren't ill, are you?" She considered her for a moment. "I'm sure it was the ship. You ought to have traveled by land."

Did her mother ever stop talking? Eleanor allowed herself to be led inside the keep, not bothering to correct her mother. All she wanted to do was rest and regain her senses.

Once inside her bedchamber, Eleanor summoned her friend Joan de Munchensi to her side and sent her other ladies away.

"I am sick as a dog. Is there nothing I can do to ease this nausea? Without the need of a physician?"

"You are with child are you not?" Joan de Munchensi asked in a barely audible whisper.

Eleanor wanted to deny it, but she couldn't lie to her. "Yes, but no one must know. Swear it."

"I swear," she said with solemnity. "But you ought to see a midwife. Perhaps there is something—"

"No." Eleanor shook her head. "Edward would catch wind of it and then he would forbid me to travel."

"As any good husband would."

Eleanor scoffed. "What point would there be in giving

146

birth to an heir if they have nothing to inherit? No. My priority is to help Edward safeguard the kingdom."

"If you insist," Joan de Munchensi said, though it was clear she was fighting her impulse to argue. "Stick to plain foods. Bread dipped in broth, hard cheese. That might help. But above all else, you need to rest. It will pass. I found the early months were the hardest."

"Thank you." Eleanor nodded. "Can I ask you for another favor? Will you ask my mother to come to me? I have no desire to dine in the great hall. She must be made to understand how dire our need is. In the meantime, I will rest."

Joan de Munchensi rested a hand on her shoulder. "Of course."

Eleanor was awoken by a soft knock on her door. For a moment she couldn't recall where she was. The tapestries on the wall were strange, as was the divan she had dozed off on. Then everything came flooding back and she rubbed the sleep from her eyes.

"Come in," she called.

Her mother strode in carrying a tray laden with pies, fruit and nuts.

"I thought you'd be hungry."

Eleanor glanced out the window. The sun was setting. "Why was I allowed to sleep so long?"

Her mother smiled down at her. "I commanded them to let you rest. Though I must say your attendants didn't need much convincing. You are as stubborn as your father."

She reached out to her, but Eleanor instinctively flinched away. Sadness shadowed her mother's features and she busied herself arranging her voluminous skirts. Eleanor caught sight of beautifully embroidered silk slippers. For all her mother's claims of poverty, there was certainly a lot of wealth all around her.

"It is the fate of all royal mothers to be strangers to their children," her mother began, taking a seat beside Eleanor. "Once our children are born, they are handed off to the wet nurse and nursemaids who see them through the struggles of childhood. Then they are sent off to cement alliances through marriages. Especially daughters. It was the fate of my mother and hers before her. It was your fate too. Our privilege is also a curse. I am sorry we are strangers to each other. Foolishly, I hoped my sons would always be close to me. At least they wouldn't be sent away from their home — but I never considered that I might be forced to remain in France while they are still in Castile." She gave a shake of her head.

Eleanor couldn't bear to meet her eyes. They'd been separated because of her mother's foolish involvement in a plot against her half-brother in the early days of his reign. But there was no point in bringing that up now. What was done was done.

"We have a chance to get to know each other now," said the Countess. "You are more than welcome to take refuge here with me. One day this will be your land to govern."

"Lady Mother, I appreciate your kind offer, but I cannot abandon my husband. I promised to bring him men to fight for him, and I will not break that promise for all the riches in the world."

"It is a man's duty to fight, not ours," her mother sniffed.

Eleanor remained staunch in the face of such opposition. "I will not be moved. If you cannot provide me with the help I need, then I will go elsewhere. But if you wish for your sacrifice to mean anything, and for you to see me crowned as Queen of England, you have to help me now."

Her mother bit her lower lip, her posture was stiff as she considered her words. "I wasn't exaggerating when I said that money is tight. I will try to help you, but I am already heavily in debt."

At Eleanor's frown, her mother smiled sorrowfully. "I'm afraid I wasn't ever good at managing finances. There never seems to be enough money so I borrow as much as I can to see us through. I have my dignity to consider. But none of that matters. You are right. You are my daughter and heir to Ponthieu. I will see what I can do for you. Eat something and we will talk more tomorrow."

"I am fine to talk now," Eleanor said, struggling to get to her feet, but she faltered as a dizzy spell overtook her.

"You are exhausted. A good night's rest will do you a world of good. Allow me to take care of you as a mother should."

Unable to summon the strength to argue, Eleanor sunk back into the cushioned divan with a sigh and a silent prayer that she had not wasted her time coming here.

The following day, her mother summoned her council, and she and Eleanor explained Eleanor's predicament. Many grumbled at the thought of raising levies for her. In response, Eleanor pointed out that the French King was helping the English cause. As her future vassals, they owed her their allegiance.

"Once we have overthrown the rebels, my husband and I shall repay any of your expenses and more. To seal this pledge, I offer you this ring," she said, pulling off a ruby ring from her finger. "It bears my seal."

"It is a pretty gesture, but it would not pay for the men you require," one lord said.

They continued to haggle, until at last it was settled that a retinue of sixty archers and twenty foot soldiers would set out with her. It was not the large force she'd hoped to raise, but Eleanor had little to barter with.

It disgusted Eleanor that her mother had given away so much of her money and power in exchange for a few luxuries. Her palace was richly furnished and they had a large deer park, and a wardrobe that would have been the envy of even Queen Alienor, but it was her vassals that ruled Ponthieu. Eleanor swore to herself that she would never trade away her power and influence for earthly comforts.

Two days later, with her companions at her side and a small army at her back, Eleanor set sail for England, where she was to meet up with Edward and his forces.

She prayed to the Virgin Mary to see her safely home and into the arms of her husband. And for her to protect the growing life in her womb.

CHAPTER 11

1264, ENGLAND

E leanor arrived in London to find the mood in the city
tense and quiet. Most troubling of all, fresh rebellion
was brewing in Wales. But for once she felt welcomed by
her father-in-law and the royalist party.

King Henry wanted Edward to lead an army into the
region and put an end to this once and for all. However,
doing so would leave them unprotected from the Barons
who were on the verge of declaring outright war with the
Crown. Even with the Flemish mercenaries Queen Alienor
had sent and the bolstering of their ranks by Eleanor, they
were stretched too thin.

By now Eleanor's pregnancy could no longer be hidden,
and while it was a cause for celebration, she couldn't help
but notice how it had unsettled Edward.

"What is on your mind, my love?" Eleanor asked,
stroking his head. They were lying side by side on their bed
watching for the first signs of dawn.

"I worry about you and the child. A country at war is no place to have a child."

She kissed his brow. "Your concern touches me. But I am at risk wherever I am. Childbirth is dangerous even in the most ideal of circumstances. Besides, even an unscrupulous man like Simon de Montfort wouldn't attack a pregnant woman. He won't harm me or this child." She placed his hand on her abdomen so he could feel the swell of her belly. "You are the one who must keep safe. We cannot bear to lose you."

He pulled her tight against him. Entwined as they were, his strength and warmth filled her with hope.

In March, King Henry wished for the lords to swear fealty to Edward as the heir apparent, but they refused unless both King Henry and Prince Edward signed the Provisions of Oxford and handed over control of the royal castles.

King Henry was ready to capitulate, but Edward refused such unfavorable terms.

"I can always retract my promises," King Henry said. "I am their anointed King. The Pope himself has declared that my word is law and that they can't dictate terms to me."

"But father, they will use this to undermine your power. We won't have a strategic stronghold to use to defend ourselves."

"They would not dare bar the gates to me."

"That is exactly what they will do," Edward said. He glanced in Eleanor's direction and they shared an exasperated look.

King Henry hated war and conflict above all else. He loved to make promises and rescind them when it suited him. Yet for all that, he believed he was owed absolute obedience. Even with his son and half-brothers arguing against his course of action he seemed determined to chart his own course.

"Father, if you give up the castles we will be placing ourselves in the hands of Simon de Montfort. We will be powerless against him."

"I agree with the Prince," Guy said, looking to his brother William for support. Now that the King needed their military prowess, the Lusignans were back in royal favor. "It is better we hold on to all that we can and shore up our defenses than capitulate."

"My Lord," William said, coming forward. "Parliament's oath of fealty to the Prince is meaningless. The whole world knows Edward is your heir. These Barons are rebels. Their word counts for nothing. Giving them what they want will not prevent them from breaking their vows."

King Henry sprang to his feet in a red rage. "I am King! I will have peace. Enough." He staggered back. "Enough of this madness and war. I am done." He slashed the air with his arm.

The room was stunned into silence. No one dared move, until at last King Henry fell back into his seat and motioned with his hand. "Go. I wish to be alone now."

The others, frustrated but unable to contradict a king, did as he bid, but Edward remained where he stood. He regarded his father's hunched form with a mixture of frustration and pity.

Eleanor approached him and, touching Edward's hand, urged him to come away. "He's tired. Let us go."

He looked at her as though she had betrayed him.

"We will carve our own path," she whispered, and at last he let himself be led away.

Once they were in the privacy of his chamber, Edward raged. "He will lose everything because he is weak. Was he always such a coward?"

Eleanor poured him a glass of wine. "Drink."

"And how will this help?"

"It will give you something to do while you think of a proper plan. The truth is, your father has been tired for a long time. He is likely to give in to Simon de Montfort's demands. But that doesn't mean you cannot act."

He considered her. "It is clear that Simon's ambitions stretch further than mere reform of government. I won't ally myself with him again."

"I wouldn't wish you to. But you can forge your own path. You are not as powerless as you imagine. We have the Flemish mercenaries, and my men from Ponthieu. Not to mention the many other men who would rally to your cause if you asked them to. Especially on behalf of your father."

"They've never rallied in the past. If anything they may turn around and accuse me of trying to usurp the throne."

"I am certain your mother would see things differently this time. She will encourage you. Write to her and ask for her permission, if you feel you must."

"As though I were a child?" Edward froze mid-step. "You are teasing me."

She grinned at him. "If anything, I'm trying to goad you

into action. The Crown needs a strong leader. That man is you."

Edward paced around his room. "I will not be the one who draws the first blade. If Simon wants war, then he shall be the one to make the first move. That way no one can claim he was merely defending himself. I must find a way to stop my father from surrendering out castles. It is a folly to do so."

Eleanor bit her lower lip when an idea struck her. "That was an agreement your father made. Not you."

His brows furrowed. Then he chuckled at her insinuation.

"They cannot accuse me of defying the terms of an agreement I have not signed. If they complain then I will claim to be ignorant of the terms." Edward fell silent as he considered this plan. "We should ride to Windsor as soon as possible."

"We?"

"I won't leave you here," he said, wrapping his arms around her. "My father is determined to sit idly by. I'd be leaving you to the wolves."

"You think Simon could take the city?"

"The Londoners hate my family, especially my mother. They hear the rumors about how she is raising another army in France, and they think she is going to bring devastation upon them. I don't trust London to remain loyal to us, especially if Simon sparks the flame of fear."

Eleanor pulled away and sank into one of the cushioned seats. "So war has come. I've been expecting it for so long, but somehow I didn't think I would actually face it. And to think this is just the beginning."

"Planning for it and seeing it are two different things."
He kneeled before her. "I will protect you and our child
with my life."

"I know," she said, wiping at the corners of her eyes.

"Rest assured that although tensions are running high,
there might still be a way to salvage this. There are no
armies in the field. Not yet."

She looked away from him. "The moment Simon
returns from his diplomatic meeting with King Louis, he
will begin his conquest."

Edward shrugged. "Perhaps we can dissuade him. Especially if I manage to shore up our position. My father must
be roused from this state of inertia."

Eleanor shook her head. "We don't need him. The men
will follow you. You are the king in all but name."

The smile that broke across his features was sad. "If that
is so, then you are a queen as well."

"Don't jest."

"I am not," he said, taking her hands in his. "You are the
queen of my heart."

She chuckled. "If your men could see what a romantic
you are, they would stop revering you as a brave warrior."

The following day, without asking the King's permission,
they left for Windsor. The Lusignan brothers stayed with
the King, but William sent his wife with Eleanor.

"You will keep my wife safe, won't you, Princess?"

"I swear it," Eleanor said, reining in her anxious horse.

"Good. Godspeed," William said, before turning to Lady Joan for a private farewell.

They left immediately, hoping Simon de Montfort and his followers would not have discovered their plans yet.

Despite the smile upon her lips, Eleanor was nervous. On the road, they could easily be ambushed. So she pushed herself to ride hard for the safety of Windsor Castle, where they could barricade themselves in the stone fortress.

Thankfully, despite the rough road, they made good time. Even the steward of the castle, a man named Richard Barnes, was taken aback by their arrival, but he didn't bar them from entering.

"My Prince, is there something I can help you with? This visit is an honor," the steward said, bowing respectfully, even while his eyes darted about, glancing furtively at the armed men that had accompanied him.

"There is disquiet in the realm," Edward said, removing his leather gloves. "As I'm sure you know. I plan to hold this castle on behalf of my father and your King. Do you have any objections?"

"N-no, of course not. I am a loyal subject," Richard said, tripping over himself as he slowly backed away.

Eleanor stepped in to intercede. "You must excuse my husband. He does not mean to accuse you. These are dangerous times." She paused to glance around the courtyard and was pleased to see it had been kept tidy. It spoke of the steward's good management. "I am sure you will prove to be a boon to the Prince as he begins his campaign and, of course, you will be rewarded handsomely for your service."

"My Lady." The steward bowed again.

Eleanor bit her lip to keep from laughing. The poor man was beside himself and she didn't want to insult him.

Together, she and Lady Joan led the women inside to find suitable quarters for themselves. Their unexpected arrival had sent the small retinue of servants left to keep the castle running into a frenzy. Shutters were flung open to allow fresh air into the rooms and covers were removed from furniture.

In the main royal apartments, the dust was particularly heavy and made Eleanor sneeze fiercely.

"Perhaps it's best we wait in the great hall?" Lady Joan suggested.

Eleanor glanced around. Her feet were swollen, and she'd hoped she'd be able to rest in a bed, but that would clearly be impossible any time soon.

"We can call more people to prepare your rooms, My Lady," one of the maids said, curtseying.

She was tempted, but she thought of how Edward wanted to shore up their supplies and would need all the manpower he could get.

"There's no need. I will wait. I'm sure we will find something to do for a few hours."

It had been difficult for Eleanor to ride, even though she had pushed through it for Edward's sake. However, the journey had taken its toll, and now she had to lean on Lady Joan while they made their way down the winding staircase. There was just as much chaos in the great hall as in the rest of the castle, but at least there was somewhere to sit.

"Let me find us something to eat," Joan said, and hurried off.

Eleanor rested back against the high-backed chair she

had found and closed her eyes to the noise and chaos. She forced herself to steady her breathing and tried to take account of the day's events.

They had made it to Windsor, and that in itself was a minor victory.

The castle was well provisioned, and Edward had sent out his men to gather more supplies from the surrounding villages and towns. They would be well garrisoned and prepared for a siege if it came to that.

Edward had chosen wisely. Here at least they were safer than at Westminster, in the heart of London. Had it never concerned Queen Alienor how much the common people hated her? Eleanor supposed not. From what she knew, Alienor was a proud woman who thought she was above reproach. Well, the hatred she had allowed to fester in the hearts of the English people might lead to her losing everything.

Despite Edward's confidence, there was no telling what the next few months would bring. Would she be widowed by this impending war? Would her child be born a pauper?

She could only pray.

After Joan brought them warm stew and they had eaten their fill, Eleanor led the ladies of her household to the castle chapel, where they prayed for the defeat of Simon de Montfort.

CHAPTER 12

1264, ENGLAND

News of their garrisoning Windsor Castle traveled fast. Less than three days later, they received a formal letter from Parliament decrying Prince Edward's act of hostility and disobedience. They reminded him that the treaty the King had signed meant that all royal castles were to be relinquished to the Lords. No one in the royal family could take possession of a castle unless given express permission to do so.

Edward stared at the messenger with such fury that the poor man looked ready to faint.

"You are lucky the rules of chivalry prevent me from running you through with my blade, for that is exactly what I wish to do." Edward tore the letter with its seal in half, and cast the pieces at the messenger's feet. "Parliament cannot dictate terms to me, a Prince of this realm."

"I-I... Forgive me, Your Grace." The messenger fell to his knees. "I was merely sent here—"

"Should I have you arrested? What if you came carrying this letter as a mere pretense to get inside our walls and spy on us?"

"My Prince, I swear to you I am innocent."

Eleanor wished to intervene, but Edward gave her no chance.

"If you are truly a loyal subject you will stop doing Parliament's bidding. Instead, you will tell me all you know about what they are doing and then go to the King in London and beg for forgiveness."

"My Prince, what do you wish to know?"

"Who sent you to carry this message?"

While the messenger fumbled for an answer, Eleanor stepped forward. "My Lord, perhaps our guest would like some refreshment. We cannot blame him for being so tongue tied while he's so exhausted, can we? You must have ridden far."

"All the way from Dover, My Lady," he said.

"Ah." Eleanor shared a look with Edward who, seeing the wisdom in her approach, stepped back.

A servant came forward with a tray of bread and ale. Eleanor invited the messenger to sit and eat, all the while plying him with questions.

They discovered that Simon de Montfort was on his way back from France, but in the meantime, his supporters were eager to find a way to remove Edward from Windsor.

At length they released the messenger. Edward wrote a letter reminding Parliament of his rights to Windsor Castle, and that if they wished to remove him, then they would have to do so by force. As Prince, it was his prerogative to do as he pleased. Only the King could command him.

Edward and Eleanor stood on the castle parapet watching the messenger ride away.

"It won't delay them too long," Edward said. "Next time, they will send an army."

"What do you plan to do?"

"I am waiting for a message from William. If he and Guy have convinced my father of the desperate need to act, then I will ride to Northampton. If we succeed in capturing that town, then we will have struck at the heart of Simon's power base. With nowhere to retreat to, it will be easier to route him."

"And what part does Windsor play in all of this?"

"We will need a safe haven to ensure our men have the supplies they need and a place to retreat to when necessary. I am charging you to keep it safe for me."

She laughed lightly. "You are making me your commander?" she teased.

"My most fearsome one. Can you do it? Can you hold the castle even if you are besieged by an army?"

"Yes. I swear I shall not open the gates to our enemies; they shall have to break them down. But I hope it doesn't come to that."

Edward nodded. "I hope God will grant us a quick victory. If my mother is successful in France and brings a large force, then we shall be safe."

"The people will hate us if we allow a French army to land on our shores."

He frowned at her words but didn't deny it. "I cannot please everyone. In time, they will forgive us. All that matters is we safeguard the throne for our children."

Eleanor nodded.

Despite their quick action to garrison Windsor, winds and bad weather brought everything to a standstill. Negotiations on both sides were fierce, but open war had not been declared.

In March, Edward felt secure enough to take his men and march to Wales to ferret out the army of Prince Llewelyn. They were gathering in larger numbers again, and the threat to the English was growing greater.

Eleanor had her own battle to face in the darkened room of her confinement chamber. She had sent Edward off with her blessing, but as her labor pains began, she wished he was near at hand.

"I am going to die," she cried out, as another spasm hit her.

Joan wiped her brow with a linen cloth dipped in cool water. "No, you are not. This is natural."

"What could be natural about this?" Eleanor asked. She didn't hear Joan's reply as another contraction came. The midwife exclaimed that she could see the head.

"It's almost done now, Princess."

"Be strong," Joan urged her.

Eleanor tightened her grip on Joan's hand and pushed.

The babe was born with a loud cry, and Eleanor sank back into the bed with relief.

"A bonny princess, My Lady," the midwife declared as she cut the cord.

"Bring her to me," Eleanor said to Joan.

The new princess, swaddled in white linen, was a bawling mess.

"We will wash her," Joan said, perhaps noting Eleanor's hesitation. "She's going to be a beauty."

Eleanor nodded. She had hoped that seeing her daughter for the first time would fill her with such overwhelming joy that the pain of the birth would disappear. But all she could think about was how she now had yet another creature to defend. To be born in such uncertain times could not be indicative of a bright future.

Despite these gloomy thoughts, Eleanor was determined to move mountains to ensure that her daughter was kept from all uncertainty and danger.

Eleanor's daughter was baptized Katherine, in a small ceremony in the chapel at Windsor. Joan stood as godmother and gifted the little princess a chain of delicate gold that had been hers when she was young.

They dared not venture beyond the castle walls for fear Simon de Montfort's forces would capture them.

Edward sent Eleanor furs and promises of returning home soon. He rejoiced in the news of her safe deliverance and the birth of their daughter. He longed for the day he could see them both.

Eleanor had always feared she was barren, and would be forced to step aside so Edward could take a new wife. The miracle of their daughter should have left her feeling elated, but though Eleanor loved her and took great pains to ensure she had every comfort, she felt despondent every time she saw her. Katherine was a reminder of everything they had to lose.

Windsor was not their home, and even her position as Princess was in jeopardy as Simon continued to gather support. The threat of danger was increasing every day, and Edward's victories in Wales were only spurring Simon's supporters into action.

Then, without warning, Edward appeared at the gates in the middle of the night. Eleanor herself had to verify that it was indeed her husband.

Beneath the travel-stained cloak, rugged beard and mud, she saw his unmistakable blue eyes.

"Open the gates, you fools," she cried out, half-laughing and half-crying as he stepped through into the courtyard and lifted her high into the air.

"I appreciate your caution, my love," he said.

"Oh Edward, you are filthier than a peasant. Come inside and I will order them to prepare a bath."

"I would like to see our daughter."

"And scare her half to death?" Eleanor scrunched up her nose. "Not to mention who knows what diseases you carry with you."

"You are the only one I'd let order me about this way. Very well, a bath it is, but you shall tell me all your news while I scrub this grime off me."

"You strike a hard bargain," she said, then despite her aversion to the dirt, she kissed him. "I missed you so much. I could barely sleep not knowing if you were alive. Whenever your letters were delayed, nightmares would plague me that Simon had captured you and held you prisoner."

"Hush, now," he whispered. "We are together again and that is all that matters."

"I know, I know," she said as she led him inside.

As he bathed, she listened to his news. The campaign in

166

Wales was going well, all things considered, but they would not have a decisive victory if England was not at peace.

"I suspect Simon's gold paid for the weapons the Welsh carried. It would certainly suit him if I and the marcher lords were distracted in Wales and didn't have time to help my father in London."

"So why have you come back?"

"William wrote to me. It has come to it at last. Tomorrow I ride to Northampton to meet up with my father's forces. We will take the city and Simon's castle."

Eleanor gaped at him. "Surely you can rest here another day?"

Edward shook his head. "No. One night's rest in your arms will be enough to reinvigorate me. My men need fresh horses, and I came hoping to bolster our numbers with more volunteers from among the commoners."

She clutched her hands in her lap.

"What?"

"I don't think we are as popular here as we once were. The mercenaries raid the countryside for food and goods. The mayor complained they were causing fights and harassing the townspeople."

Edward didn't seem surprised. "They are impatient for war. But now I shall give it to them. Don't worry. I will ensure that everyone is repaid. For now I don't care if I few peasants lost a cow or a few men earned some bruises."

Eleanor wanted to argue but bit her tongue. Her husband could be callous. But in uncertain times like these, it was a necessary evil. They couldn't afford to be generous and kind.

After Edward had washed and changed into a robe of

heavy wool dyed a dark blue, he allowed Eleanor to lead him to the makeshift nursery.

The nursemaid and wet nurse curtseyed politely as they went about their business.

Katherine was awake in her cradle, having just fed. Her eyes were already half closing when Edward picked her up.

"Gently, my love," Eleanor said.

He adjusted his hold to support her head and placed a tender kiss on her cheek, which Katherine did not approve of. She scrunched up her little face, ready to cry. Without needing to be told, he laughed and rocked her in his arms. "There now, I promise you I shall shave this shaggy beard of mine." Then, looking up at Eleanor, said, "What a perfect princess you have made for us."

Eleanor's heart leaped at the praise.

"I am sorry I cannot spend more time with the two of you," Edward said, fighting back a yawn. The nursemaid came forth and took the princess from his arms.

He gave his daughter one last blessing and left the nursery with Eleanor.

"I am a restless man, but I have seen tonight the bliss that comes from the simple joys of holding my child in my arms. Oh, Eleanor, if only I could safeguard this kingdom for us. Then we might have that tranquility for the rest of our days."

"I don't believe that is to be our fate," Eleanor said ruefully. "Even if there wasn't Simon de Montfort to contend with, there will always be Wales, or Scotland, and even France. Can we even hope for peace in such a time?"

He chuckled. "No, I don't suppose we can. But we can dream."

"It may lead to disappointment."

He regarded her. "Eleanor, what is this? You are shrouded in darkness. Never have I heard you speak so."

"Fear has its talons in me, and I don't know if it shall ever release me," she confessed.

He embraced her and held her tight as first the tears came and then the sobs that wracked her whole body. There, in the empty corridor, they stood until all her tears had been spent.

Only when she pulled away did she realize he had shed tears of his own. "I know how my father is feeling. A part of me is tired too. Tired of Englishman fighting against Englishman. Tired of being a laughing stock. Tired of feeling weak and unable to command our own people. But there's another side of me that is burning up with rage. I will show the world I am not one to be disregarded. They shall learn to fear me."

She shuddered at his words, but Eleanor felt it too — the growing frustration that ate away at her, threatening to break her.

He let out a heavy breath and she felt him slump against her. "After this is all over, I have sworn I will take up the cause and join the holy war. Then at least I shall be absolved of the sin of killing my fellow countrymen and laying waste to my own country."

"Where you go, I will go too."

He looked like he wished to argue, but he didn't forbid her.

The following day she dressed in her finest gown, taking extra care with her toilette. Everything had to be perfect. The wet nurse carrying Katherine, swaddled in a silk blanket of royal purple, followed behind her as the household went to bid Edward farewell.

He was a blaze of black and gold. A fresh steed had been provided from the stables with a coat as black as night. His armor had been cleaned and polished overnight and now it reflected the sun. Edward was taller than any other man and far more regal. There was no denying her husband was a prince among men.

He saluted them and extracted one further promise from her that she would keep his castle and child safe. With that he led his men away to war.

Eleanor watched them go, her hand reaching for Joan's as they watched them disappear from view. Joan was fighting back tears while her other hand caressed the swell of her stomach. She was to have another child in a few months and hadn't had the chance to see her husband before he rode off to war. Eleanor pitied her.

"In a few weeks we will be feasting at Westminster and all of this will be forgotten," Eleanor said, though she doubted her own words.

While the men went to war, the women would have to be satisfied with the banal tasks of everyday life. They might prepare poultices for wounds, gather supplies for the army or take care of the children, but Eleanor knew it wouldn't provide respite from the dreary task of waiting.

With a sigh of resignation, Eleanor and Joan retreated inside.

CHAPTER 13

1264, ENGLAND

Summer was fast approaching. Already in mid-April the sun felt unbearable. The last messages Eleanor received from Edward were to let her know he had met up with his father's forces. He reminded her to stay alert, and even though Simon de Montfort would hardly to bother making war on two women, there could still be trouble.

Then, at last, good news reached them. The King's forces, commanded by Edward, had captured Northampton. In one fell swoop, he'd shown the strength of royalist party and shaken the Barons' confidence.

Unfortunately the victory made Simon take him seriously too. In retribution, he led an army to lay siege to Rochester Castle.

Eleanor received a note from Edward, and read it out loud to Joan. *"By the time you receive this we will be on our way to Rochester to help relieve our friends. We are in good spirits. Everyone is well. We've received money from my mother in France. I love you."*

"Don't worry," Eleanor consoled Joan, who was beside herself with worry. "Your husband is alive and well."

"But he's going into yet another battle. How many more will there be before this is done?" she sobbed.

Eleanor gripped her by the shoulders. "Joan, you cannot let yourself succumb to grief. Think of your son and the baby growing in your womb. Your family needs you to be strong. Life will be full of battles that our husbands must face, and when they grow, your sons as well."

Joan wiped the tears from her eyes. "You are right. Of course. I let myself get carried away."

"It is hard to be here, apart from our husbands, but they need us to hold this castle for them and so we shall."

The quiet that followed news of the army's move south should have been disconcerting. However, managing the castle distracted Eleanor so much that she hadn't realized how much time had passed until a messenger appeared at the gate.

It was Edward's own squire, looking grave and exhausted. He fell to his knees before her and Eleanor feared the worst.

"Tell me quickly," she commanded him.

"The King and my master, Prince Edward, engaged Simon de Montfort's forces at Lewes. They were caught unaware and had no choice but to fight. They lost. Both are alive but captured by the traitor."

Joan pushed to the forefront of the group. "And my husband? What of William?"

"Alive as well. But Lord Guy perished in battle. God rest his soul."

"Amen." Both Joan and Eleanor crossed themselves. While the news was tragic, they had feared even worse. Both women shuddered at how close death had brushed by their husbands. And now they had to face an uncertain future.

"Tell me more," Eleanor said, urging the man to his feet. "What has become of the royal forces? Do you have some message for me?"

"None, My Lady. Before the battle, Prince Edward commanded me to come to you directly should we lose. I have done as he asked but he gave me no instructions on what to tell you."

Eleanor nodded. "Very well. I shall do as my husband commanded and hold Windsor Castle for him." She called out to the rest of the men so they might all hear. "We shall never surrender while we have breath left in our lungs. For we are loyal English men and women!"

An answering cry rang out around the courtyard.

Once the squire had been fed and given fresh clothes, Eleanor invited him into her presence chamber where the castle chamberlain and steward waited.

"Please sit; we need you to tell us everything so we might better prepare for the coming days."

She had a pen at the ready to record all he said, for Eleanor did not trust her own mind at the moment.

After the news of the King's capture, Eleanor refused to allow anyone to leave or enter the castle. They lived as if already under siege, and she ensured her remaining knights and soldiers patrolled the castle walls day and night. The last thing she wanted was to be caught unawares.

Two weeks after the Battle of Lewes, a messenger, accompanied by a small force of men, came from Simon de Montfort, demanding she surrender the castle and come to London.

Eleanor sneered at him. "You do not have the men to compel me to open the gates. I would be a fool to throw myself upon Simon de Montfort's mercy."

"My Lady, your husband and father-in-law are already in custody. They are safe in Lord Simon's care. The King has signed over his royal prerogative and now you ought to obey Lord Simon as you would have obeyed the King."

Eleanor's peel of laughter echoed all around the gathered men. "I would be a fool to take your word for it."

"I have here Lord Simon's seal and formal declaration."

Eleanor cocked her head. "And I am to believe him? He could be lying. Maybe he was defeated at Lewes and this is all an elaborate trap. No, you will have to return to your master empty handed. I'm afraid I will not be going anywhere with you."

He looked frustrated, but what could he do, especially when faced with a row of angry archers on the wall, bows at the ready.

"This won't be the last you've heard of me."

She strode away with her head held high, but she knew he was right. Simon would come with his army and lay siege to Windsor. How long could they endure inside these walls with no hope of salvation?

Anxiety was high, but the way she stood up to the messenger had emboldened the men garrisoning the castle. They mocked Simon de Montfort for being too afraid to face a woman. Yet for all their jests they knew they were running on borrowed time. The day of reckoning was coming. And soon.

Eleanor prayed for a miracle, but none came.

Their supplies were dwindling fast and Eleanor limited herself to a diet of plain gruel, so the children might have some meat with their dinners.

As predicted, Simon de Montfort himself appeared at the head of his army, bearing a letter from the King and her husband. It was an official command to surrender the castle and return to Westminster with Simon. She was to order the mercenaries to disband and send away the Gascon levies and archers from Ponthieu. If they came now, they would all be given safe passage home.

Seeing the cause was lost, Eleanor knew there was no point in prolonging this. Not that she could have refused a direct order from the King.

She stood proudly in the courtyard, dressed in a gown of fine white cloth, a circlet on her head, flanked by Joan and other members of her household. Arranging her face in an expression of serene indifference, she gave the command to open the drawbridge.

Every click of the heavy chain that lifted the portcullis was like a blow to her very soul. She had never imagined that giving herself up as a prisoner would be this difficult.

Simon de Montfort rode in and regarded her coolly. "I

am glad you have come to your senses, My Lady. There is no need for any further bloodshed or theatrics."

"There never needed to be any. If only you had not designs on the throne yourself, then all this could've been avoided," she said, unconcerned about the rage on his face even as he rode towards her, as though he might charge at her.

Eleanor didn't falter or step back; she stood defiant.

He stopped short of her, but leaned over in the saddle to stare her down. "My Lady, you are foolish if you think you can accuse me of wrongdoing. At one time your husband and I were in agreement. Corruption is rife in the kingdom and a greedy witch of a queen sacked it of its riches and handed out parcels of land to her friends and family. This stops now."

Eleanor remained tightlipped and he pulled back, scoffing. "Play the part of the noble lady if you wish. But you are returning to London with me. I promise you and your household shall be treated with all the respect you deserve."

Eleanor bit her cheek. She wondered how much more he would've preferred to just kill the royal family and claim the throne for himself. But the very same rules that constrained him, empowered her.

Simon had planned ahead — a litter was waiting for Eleanor and Katherine. As they were shepherded around and the servants instructed to pack her clothing and items, Eleanor noticed there were two separate cavalcades.

"Are we going our separate ways?" Eleanor asked Simon, unable to keep the hope from her voice.

His smile was rueful. "No. I am here to personally

escort you to Westminster. The Countess of Pembroke is to retire to a nunnery."

"What?" Eleanor's eyes widened. It was the first time she'd shown genuine surprise.

"It is the cost of her defiance. She will not be harmed, you have my word."

"Your word counts for nothing," Eleanor snapped.

His eyes were dark with rage. "And what do you have to say for your husband? Did he not trick monks into opening the doors of their monastery only for him to pillage their gold? Could you claim he is an honest, godly man?" He spat on the ground. "Careful with your accusations, My Lady."

Eleanor stiffened and fought to appear stoic.

From the corner of her eye, she saw the wet nurse being escorted to the litter with Katherine in her arms. Eleanor felt a pang of fear for her child. Would she be taken away too?

Elsewhere, Joan had been bundled into another litter. Eleanor rushed to her side to bid farewell. Her poor friend was in no condition to ride. She was sick with worry, as there was still no word about the whereabouts of her husband. All they knew was that he had not died.

"If I hear anything I shall write to you."

"I think there's a reason they aren't telling me," Joan sobbed. "He's on his deathbed or he's been thrown into some dungeon and left to rot."

"I don't believe that. Given their jubilant mood, I'm sure they'd tell you," Eleanor said. "I'll try to discover what has happened to him for you. At least you'll be comfortable and in good hands, whereas I will be at the mercy of the council."

"I'll pray for you. Stay safe."

The two women embraced one last time.

The sun had set by the time Simon's men had stripped the castle bare. Yet that didn't prevent them from setting off. Using torches to light the way they set off.

In spite of her anxiety the journey passed quickly, and she was within sight of London before she could even begin to process the events of the day.

When they arrived at Westminster, Eleanor and her daughter were taken to the royal apartments and locked inside.

"What of my husband?" she asked. "When will I see him?"

"All in due course," replied Simon. "If you need anything you need only ask one of the guards and they will try to assist you."

"Am I to be a prisoner here? Because if so, then I would prefer a swift execution."

"You are distressed so I will let you rest after your hard journey. I pray that you will have the good sense to make peace with the situation you are in." And with a courteous bow he left her.

Eleanor took a moment to see that the wet nurse and her daughter were settled in before exploring the apartments they'd been allotted.

The tapestries had been left untouched, but there was no sign of her jewelry or finer clothes. She found a few plain gowns inside chests, as well as linen and other necessities, but Simon had essentially robbed her. Was his own wife wearing the looted treasures now? Eleanor, not normally one to ill-wish someone, found herself hoping his wife would choke on her pearls.

CHAPTER 14

1264, ENGLAND

The days dragged on and on. While Eleanor knew she should be grateful for the luxurious trappings, she was still imprisoned, and took to pacing around the chamber like an angry cat. Food and drink were brought in for them at regular intervals, and servants came to stoke the fire and tidy around the rooms, but they never spoke to her, nor would she trust anything they had to say. Simon would ensure that only those loyal to himself and his cause were allowed access to her.

A month went past before, Edward was allowed to see her.

He held her at arm's length, examining her for any injury.

"I am alright," she said with a laugh.

"That is good." Edward looked relieved but still on edge.

"What is the matter? I mean, besides our obvious

imprisonment and the fact we are kept as little better than hostages."

"You are to be sent to Canterbury with my father. They will keep me under arrest at Wallingford to ensure we are separated. I am sure they believe if we were together, we would plot our escape."

"Oh, Edward, I thought they would keep us together at the very least. Why has the council allowed this cruelty?"

"Simon holds sway over them. They will obey him and set my father up as a puppet king. We will be kept as hostages to ensure no one else rises in rebellion against them. I'm sure Simon would prefer if some accident befell us, but for now we are useful to him."

"Don't say such things," Eleanor said, grasping at her crucifix.

"I speak only the truth. You must take care with your food and drink. Don't allow yourself to be drawn into any plotting; it might be a trap set by Simon to prove you are a traitor."

She nodded. They sat together, admiring their daughter and it was then that Eleanor told him of her suspicions.

"I think I am with child again." She laughed at his surprise. "I know. God has seen to make me a fertile woman at the worst possible time."

Edward kneeled before her, taking her hands in his and kissing her fingertips. "My love, I swear to you that one day we will be restored to our rightful place. All this will be forgotten."

"I believe you, Edward, I truly do. No prison can hold you for long. I also have faith that the barons will quickly lose faith in Simon. In time, they may grow greedy for power and start fighting amongst themselves. This isn't the end for us, we just have to be patient."

The intensity in his gaze as he looked up at her sent a shiver down her spine, and she knew they would ultimately emerge victorious.

Their time together was fleeting, but she'd found her strength again.

Slowly, as Simon enforced his control over the country, she was allowed more freedom. After all, she was a mere woman and in her condition, she wouldn't be able to flee.

For all his dismissals of her, Queen Alienor was still a thorn in his side. News of the army she was raising in France was coming in every day. All they were waiting for was a fair wind.

Given that King Louis continued to give Alienor sanctuary, there was nothing Simon could do but urge King Henry to write to his wife, condemning her actions. Eleanor suspected she burned the letters without reading them.

To keep herself occupied, Eleanor wrote letters to her husband and to Joan at the nunnery in Wilton. News of William finally reached her ears. He had joined Queen Alienor in France. War made strange bedfellows. The two of them were bitter enemies in the past, but were now united by a common cause.

The letters Eleanor sent were unsealed, and she didn't even attempt a hidden message, knowing Simon's men would pore over every detail hoping to find some incriminating evidence against her.

With the end of August in sight, she received news from the council that she was to move to Canterbury, along with the King.

"I don't see anything mentioning my daughter in this letter," Eleanor said.

Pity crossed the features of Lord Nicholas de Seagrave, her jailor, for a brief moment. "She is to remain here at Westminster." At Eleanor's protest he rushed to assure her. "She will be provided with every comfort and security. It will be better if she is here rather than in Canterbury." His words were laden with meaning, but she struggled to understand.

"My Lord, you must be frank with me. What is awaiting us in Canterbury?"

"Nothing you should concern yourself with, but there is still rebellion in the realm. And Queen Alienor is a constant threat. I wouldn't wish my own children to be caught up in a battle."

"I see," Eleanor said. She had little choice but to go with them and leave her daughter behind. Even if she fought them tooth and nail, they would overpower her and in the end the result would be the same. Simon was determined to take her away from all that she loved.

"If you wish to blame anyone, blame Queen Alienor. She sent secret missives to the remaining royalist supporters, and they tried to break Edward free from his prison."

Eleanor gasped. This was the first she had heard of it. "And?"

"And what, My Lady? They failed, of course. The guards threatened to catapult Prince Edward to them in pieces and they retreated. Who knows what lies the Queen told his supporters, but it would take an army many months to lay siege to the castle." Lord Nicholas caught himself before he said more and stopped to clear his throat. "Within a few hours we will be departing. I merely wished to prepare you."

"Etiquette dictates I thank you, but I find I cannot," Eleanor said, turning away from him.

On the journey to Canterbury, she traveled in a closed litter, sitting across from her father-in-law. He looked tired; the lines on his face had deepened and he kept babbling about inconsequential niceties.

"Do you think we shall be able to celebrate Christmas at Canterbury? The cathedral there is certainly beautiful, but I don't think any castle can rival the beauty of Westminster."

Eleanor ignored him; he wasn't really looking for an answer, merely for something to fill the silence. She pulled back the curtains of the litter a little to get a view of the gray sky outside. Guards flanked them on either side. There was no hope of escape or rescue. Not to mention the small army riding behind and in front of the litter.

Closing the curtain again, she regarded King Henry. "I can play the lute for you if you wish."

His eyes lit up at that and he nodded enthusiastically.

Eleanor supposed she should be grateful that Simon hadn't robbed her of all her possessions. She unwrapped the lute that had been a gift from her half-brother. The wood was intricately carved and was inset with a crown of rubies at the top. She set her fingers to the strings and drew out a beautiful uplifting song she remembered from her childhood, allowing it to transport her to the orange groves of Castile.

Life in Canterbury was monotonous. Occasionally, someone would come demanding she affixed her seal to a letter or proclamation. Whether she wanted to or not, Eleanor had no choice but to comply. She was sure her mother and the French King were smart enough to recognize her letters about Simon's righteous rule, for the lies they were.

Simon's actions outraged the Pope. He threatened the barons with excommunication if they didn't quickly restore King Henry to the throne.

However, Simon de Montfort's hold on the council was so absolute that while some may have hesitated, no one dared speak out.

Still Simon and his loyal adherents arrived in Canterbury and were discussing the matter while, King Henry was forced to write a letter to the Pope asking for him to reconsider.

Eleanor watched with disinterest as they paced around and had not moved from her seat near the fire. These days she had little energy to move about, and wondered if the child in her womb was sapping all her strength.

"Who knows what lies Queen Alienor has told him ..." Simon said, his gaze fixed on Eleanor as though daring her to contradict him. But she remained silent and compliant in her seat as she worked on her needlework. "... And how much of England's gold has been used to bribe him."

At that, Eleanor's hands stilled. Her smile was still serene as she regarded him. "Lord Simon, are you suggesting that His Holiness would succumb to bribery?"

The council murmured at her words.

Simon inclined his head. "You are right. I misspoke. I am sure his advisors and those around him are the ones who are corruptible. Therefore, I will pray that he will not listen to the foolish lies they spread about England."

"As will I and everyone else in this room," Eleanor said, and with a small sigh she returned to her needlework as though nothing was amiss.

Despite Simon's apparent confidence, the Pope's declaration created unease among the magnates that had flocked to Simon's cause. This unrest only spurred Simon to strengthen his hold on power. He began by demanding that the King summon Parliament. To ensure he had approval of the nation, he summoned four representatives from every county.

Eleanor wasn't present at the proceedings, but Simon managed to convince them to codify the Provisions of Oxford into law. The King, still a prisoner, affixed his seal to the proclamation, thus robbing himself of even more power and lands. This proclamation also robbed Eleanor of any income from the lands she received when she married Edward. She was all but destitute and was forced to rely on Simon's charity to pay for her food and servants.

She suffered this indignity well enough, but in September, tragedy struck. News was brought to her that her daughter Katherine had perished during the night.

But it was not Eleanor who shed tears — it was the King himself who, upon hearing of his granddaughter's death, convulsed into sobs.

Eleanor felt nothing but a dreadful stillness, as though she'd been frozen within her body.

"My Lady," her maid said, taking her by the hand. "Please sit down."

The lords who had come to tell her the news were grave, their discomfort evident on their faces. It was no easy thing to tell a mother her child had died. This wasn't a victory on the battlefield.

"Tell me how it happened, my lords," Eleanor said, her voice barely audible.

Lord Nicholas, who'd been her jailor at Westminster, stepped forward. "She caught a cold. Physicians and doctors were brought to her. She was recovering and they hadn't believed it was anything serious. Then in the night a fit of convulsions brought on by fever ended her life. I am sorry for this tragic loss."

Eleanor glared at him. If he was expecting her to say something to exonerate him, he would be disappointed. "It is tragic that I was separated from my daughter. She needed her mother and I was not there."

The lords bowed their heads, avoiding her cold gaze. She relished the power she held over them in this moment, but their uneasiness was insufficient punishment for the anger she felt. One day soon she would have her vengeance.

"And the funeral? Shall Lord Simon grant her one?"

"Of course, My Lady."

"Good. Then I will arrange it. If I am not allowed to attend, then the very least I can do is arrange it so my daughter will be sent to her grave as befits a princess." It was then that her voice cracked and she couldn't bear to speak anymore. However, she couldn't let them see her tears, either. It wasn't until they left that she allowed herself to cry.

How much sorrow could her heart bear?

Her maids tried to cheer her up by reminding her of the blessing she still had. But it didn't console her to know her husband was still alive and that she'd be blessed with other children. After all, these could be lost too, and it frightened her.

Eleanor fought to keep from sinking into despair, even as she planned for the future.

The King was kind to her in the days following her daughter's death. He was allowed few freedoms, but they walked together in the gardens and took solace praying in the chapel.

King Henry was not the helpless man she'd always envisioned. For all his faults he clearly he loved his family very much. He often spoke to Eleanor of his children and of his wife Alienor with such love and devotion that she began to pity him.

He was a puppet king, all his energy and vitality drained away by years of rebellion and infighting among his nobles. She tried to envision him as he must have been in his youth but failed to do so.

Nor could she find it in her heart to forgive him and his wife for the disaster they had made of their rule. If Queen

Alienor had been more circumspect about who she had favored, and how much they had taxed their people to pay for fleeting luxuries, then maybe they wouldn't have been in this position.

"We lost children too," the King said, as they walked arm in arm. "I will never forget them. It is hardest when you've seen them grow out of their infancy and you start to plan their future, only for it to be snuffed out so suddenly."

They rounded a bend and came upon a little maze garden. The guards closed ranks around them as though they feared they might escape through the hedges.

"Even if they are born sickly and you prepare yourself for the worst, it's still a shock when the end comes."

"Was that how it was for you, Your Grace, when Princess Katherine passed away? Edward mentioned how tough it had been for you both."

King Henry inclined his head. "Yes. After her second birthday her health deteriorated rapidly, but still we never gave up hope. I should not be filling your head with such sad tales. You must focus on the future."

Eleanor gazed at him sidelong. Did he know something? Or was he just trying to be optimistic?

"I have found that time heals many wrongs," he said, nodding his head sagely. "All will be as God intends."

"Amen," she said, still not brave enough to ask the all-important question.

"Soon I believe our family will be reunited."

"When?" Eleanor whispered.

He winked at her. "When God wills it."

Even as they continued their walk, Eleanor wasn't sure what to make of this but she allowed herself to hope.

With Christmas approaching, the King and Eleanor were moved once again. This time Simon took them into the heart of his lands at Woodstock. Eleanor wondered what he meant by this move, but it became clear he was merely trying to cement support among the English people.

Simon de Montfort had grown more confident as his grip on power tightened. King Henry had remained compliant all these long months and appeared to be no threat.

Eleanor was kept under heavy watch so there was nothing for her to do but focus on the child growing within her womb and try to ignore her grief.

So she was surprised to be told that Edward would be released and brought to stay with them.

"It'll be a happy reunion for you all," Simon announced cheerfully.

Eleanor's suspicions were alerted by this and she wondered what he was planning.

"I must thank you for bringing me this wonderful news," Eleanor said keeping her eyes downcast. "I have prayed to see him every day we were apart."

Simon scowled. "I am sure you prayed, My Lady, but I have no doubt you also prayed for my destruction."

"I wonder then, why you wish to bring Edward here?"

He gave her a long look. "I am not the monster you think I am. You ought to count your blessings and not complain."

Eleanor held his gaze before looking away, not deigning to answer. She could only guess that either Simon felt secure enough in his control over the country or that his council had pressured him to treat the royal family more gently. Many had disapproved of how he had refused to allow Edward to visit his daughter's grave. It had been the first sign of discontent among the barons.

CHAPTER 15

1264-1265, ENGLAND

When Edward arrived at the palace, they flew into each other's arms and she was grateful to be sleeping under the same roof as him again.

"You have changed so much," he said with a teasing laugh, placing a hand on her belly, only for his smile to deepen when he felt the child kick beneath his palm.

"That's right, you punish your father for teasing me," Eleanor said.

"You know you are as beautiful as ever, don't you? But I apologize. In the time we've been apart I seem to have forgotten my manners."

Eleanor merely took his hand and led him to the seats she had arranged before the fire. "Now that we have time, I want you to tell me everything. What happened at Lewes?"

Edward hesitated. "I have no desire to recount that terrible day."

"I need to understand. Please."

At last he relented. "Very well, but I am not proud, for I fear I am to blame."

Eleanor was ready to disagree but he silenced her with one look.

"We outnumbered Simon's forces so even though they held the higher ground we felt confident of victory. You must understand, in Wales, I faced worse odds and won. This looked like it would be an easy victory."

She reached over to squeeze his hand.

"Things were going well. A contingent of men broke away from Simon's army and I gave chase to them. It was a mistake. In the heat of the moment I had drifted too far from the main army and left my father unsupported by my cavalry. They forced the royal army into the city and there in the narrow streets our numbers meant nothing. By the time I had returned it was too late. We were forced to surrender and now we are in this predicament."

The shame in Edward's voice rattled Eleanor. "It was a mistake, but it happens to the best of all men. You cannot change the past, but you can learn from it."

"Is that what your philosophers say?"

A weak smile spread over Eleanor lips. "I have not had the pleasure of reading their essays in ages. I know my words are of little comfort but we must keep our eyes on the future. No matter how much the past might haunt us."

She touched her belly, tears pricking at the corner of her eyes as she thought of Katherine.

"I am sorry, Eleanor for everything." His words were a gentle whisper.

The reason for Edward's release quickly became clear. Simon summoned Parliament and Edward was ordered to appear before them. As he stood there, Edward was commanded to give up his claims to the earldom of Chester. His humiliation was complete when Simon invested himself with the stolen title in the very same ceremony. Edward was forced to watch as his powerless father fix his seal to the letter patent.

Despite this apparent victory, the mood in the parliament had shifted. Simon's increasing greed and cruelty displeased many.

When Edward returned to their apartments, he was like a caged lion. There was nothing Eleanor could say or do to calm him. She left him to his brooding and went to speak to King Henry, who was sitting at his desk reading from a Bible.

"Your Grace, I've come to ask you about the session of Parliament," Eleanor said, curtseying deeply. "Edward is incoherent for once and I can't get a sensible word out of him."

"He needs to control that anger of his," King Henry said wisely. He had aged in these last few months of his confinement. Streaks of white had appeared in his hair and his face was creased by new lines.

"So Simon plans to strip us of all our remaining lands and titles?"

King Henry harrumphed. "He can try. But a lion is still a lion, even if others call it a cat."

"But he can have us killed if he wishes," Eleanor said, putting a hand over her belly. "We are threats to his rule."

King Henry nodded. He seemed so unconcerned by all this that she wondered if he had lost his wits. At last he closed his Bible and regarded her kindly.

"Take a seat. You must remember to rest," he said. "Soon you will be entering confinement. Pray to God and forget the secular troubles of our world as you face your travail."

She promised to do as he bid but felt agitated by the inactivity.

"Simon is courting danger," the King murmured under his breath. It sounded more like a low hum, but Eleanor heard his words nonetheless. "He angers his supporters as he becomes more and more powerful. He is greedy and doesn't share. Many were against his decision to strip Edward of his earl-dom. He is sowing the seeds of his own destruction. Much as I have allowed this to come about by giving my wife free rein with her little projects —" His eyes crinkled at the corners in response to her incredulous expression, "— I've had lots of time to ruminate on my own failings. None of us is perfect. We are human. However, Simon is no king, and at the end of the day our bloodline with its divine right will prevail."

He stopped to cough. "Not to mention that the Pope and all of Christendom will come to our aid. No monarch wants to see a mere lord succeed at deposing another monarch." He chuckled. "It sets a bad precedent, as I'm sure you can imagine."

Eleanor inclined her head. "You give me hope."

He shook his head. "And I shouldn't have. Because it's

just as likely that I am wrong. But I don't like to see you despairing. Go to my son, see if you can make him see sense."

"I will. Thank you," Eleanor said.

"If you wouldn't mind, I would appreciate it if you stitched me a new shirt. Queen Alienor used to make me such beautiful ones, and I would like to have a new one for the Christmas feast."

"Of course, I'd be happy to," Eleanor said curtseying. Her father-in-law never failed to shock her.

———

As the year drew to a close, Simon was determined to throw a proper Christmas feast for all his adherents. Under the King's seal he summoned all the lords of the land to come celebrate with him at Woodstock.

During the rule of King Henry I, Woodstock Palace had housed the royal menagerie, and the King would entertain foreign dignitaries by taking them there for hunting expeditions and to show them the exotic animals.

The only captive creatures in the palace now were the remaining royal family. Eager to show the control he held over them, Simon commanded them to attend the feasts and celebrations.

Eleanor tried to refuse. "I should be entering my confinement," she said, motioning to her great belly. "Would you wish to be accused of mistreating me?"

He tutted. "Never — of course I would not wish for you to overtax yourself. Your midwife assured me that you don't need to enter your confinement until after the New Year. Wouldn't you rather celebrate with your husband?"

"Of course I would. But there is another reason why I could not attend."

Simon's good humor melted away. "And what is that?"

"My ladies and I have nothing suitable to wear. You have taken my dower lands and claimed my allowance from the royal treasury. I have no funds with which to purchase new clothes. I refuse to appear before the court looking like a pauper."

He wrung his hands together and through gritted teeth said, "Very well. If I send you new clothes and trinkets to wear, will you be more amenable to attending the celebrations?"

Eleanor thought for a moment. "And my ladies?"

"Yes. Yes. Don't trouble me over a few bolts of cloth," Simon said, losing his temper at last.

It amused Eleanor how easily she could make him lose his temper. It was the least she could do to repay him for all the pain and suffering he had inflicted on her and her family.

Eleanor attended Mass decked in a new gown of beautiful blue damask. She felt ungainly with her big belly, but hoped she managed to look regal as Edward led her to their seat at the high table.

Despite being shown every respect, it was clear that power lay with Simon de Montfort. He outshone both the King and Prince with the extravagance of his dress.

While Simon continued to command the attention of the room, there was an undercurrent of dissatisfaction that wasn't there before. In the past, the King was all but ignored; now many of the lords made an effort to pay their respects to the silent man.

Even more kept casting furtive glances towards Edward. Perhaps they regretted siding with Simon's faction. For all their efforts, none had benefited as much as the man himself. Indeed, perhaps the extravagance of this feast was Simon's way of placating his friends.

Eleanor watched him hand out purses of gold and other costly gifts to the visitors. They were accepted with thin smiles, but if Simon noticed he showed no sign. His spirits were high and he was determined to enjoy his victory.

———

As promised, after the Christmas feast, Eleanor retreated to her chambers to begin her confinement until her child was born. Edward escorted her and at the threshold held her back with a touch on her shoulder.

"My love, I shall be praying for you. Already I am counting the days until our child is born and I can see you again."

"Thank you, I shall be thinking of you too," Eleanor said, her smile strained. "We both face a battle."

In the darkened chambers, Eleanor felt time slow to a crawl. She dreaded a child being born at Woodstock. She'd been taken away from Katherine and hadn't been there for her in her final moments. What if this child succumbed to illness too? Her heart hammered wildly in her chest at the mere thought.

Where once her prayers might have been for a son, now she merely prayed for a healthy child that would grow into adulthood.

It didn't help her anxieties that she was served by women Simon had appointed. She didn't trust any of them and wished her request to see Lady Joan had not been denied. Eleanor felt she'd be facing childbirth alone, but she held onto that glimmer of hope the King had given her.

Joan was born in early January. She was small but fed well, and her lungs were powerful enough to wake the whole palace with her cries.

"She will be a warrior," Edward said, holding his daughter in his arms. "Was Katherine this small?"

"You only saw Katherine when she was already a month old," Eleanor reminded him. "But Joan is smaller, yes."

"She'll grow," Edward said. His words sounded more like a command than a reassurance.

"Daughter, you will have to obey your father, for he will be disappointed in you if you do not do as he says."

Edward chuckled and handed the baby back to the waiting wet nurse. Only then did he turn back to Eleanor where she lay stretched out on the bed. "And how are you? I was told the physicians were summoned to examine you."

Eleanor snorted. "For all the good that did me. But your father was kind and paid for my medications. The doctors say their draughts will strengthen me, but all they seem to do is make me vomit."

"Do as they say. You need to recover," Edward said, placing a kiss on her brow. "I need you."

She smiled up at him. "I'm not going anywhere."

Indeed, day by day she felt stronger, and though Joan's birth had been a harrowing experience, by the end of the month she was back on her feet.

In February, Simon moved them back to Westminster. Here Eleanor was once again separated from her husband, which she protested against vehemently. Eventually she was allowed to see him at Mass and was glad to see he was well.

"Trouble is brewing," Edward whispered to her one day as they kneeled before the crucifix.

But for who? Eleanor never got the chance to ask. Two weeks later, Edward and King Henry were packed off to Hereford. Simon kept them under heavy guard and ordered that Eleanor was to remain at Westminster.

"Why am I not permitted to join my husband?" she asked, all but shouting at him.

"You should be grateful I am allowing you the company of your child. Before you called me cruel for separating you."

Eleanor didn't back down even in the face of his increasing anger. Perhaps she wanted to intentionally provoke him in front of the Earl of Gloucester, who was with him. The Earl looked unsettled by the scene he was witnessing.

"Lord Simon, I pray you see sense. My family is under your control already. What harm could it do to keep me with my husband?"

"I don't need to listen to this." Simon stormed out, commanding the Earl to follow after him. "There's no reasoning with her."

Eleanor couldn't hear Gloucester's reply, but it didn't sound sympathetic.

CHAPTER 16

1265, ENGLAND

Winter gave way to spring and Eleanor spent as much time outside as she could. Even when it rained she would sit in an alcove breathing in the fresh air. As she watched the stormy clouds above, she could pretend she wasn't a prisoner.

The one benefit of being at Westminster was that she had access to the library and could spend her days immersed in study. It gave her something to do, for she had neither the funds nor permission to venture out on rides or hunts with her ladies.

Sometimes they would play cards, but they would gamble with stones or pretty ribbons rather than coins. It was a far cry from what should've been her due, but she bore it well and enjoyed herself nonetheless.

As she was sitting in the flower gardens examining the budding fruit trees, a troop of armed guards marched in.

Eleanor stood up and straightened to her full height.

"What can I help you with, Sir?" she asked their commander.

"We are ordered to take you to your apartments and you are not to leave them until we hear otherwise."

"On whose command?" Her voice was steady even as fresh fear bloomed in her chest. Had Simon decided to act against them at last?

"It doesn't matter who, Princess. You are to come with us," the soldier said. From his expression it was clear there was no point arguing with him, and Eleanor forced herself to step forward.

"Very well, as you wish. I am powerless to stop you."

With her head held high, showing no fear, she allowed herself to be escorted back to her rooms. She didn't flinch as she heard the lock turn in the door, and merely suggested to her ladies that they play some music.

Five days passed without news. The armed guards that brough their food told them nothing. On the six day, Eleanor prevailed upon one of them to tell her what had happened.

"Your husband has escaped Hereford and is raising an army in the Marches."

"He has?" Eleanor was incredulous, even as she feared the repercussions if he should fail. "Thank you for telling me."

The guard nodded but couldn't bring himself to say anything else. So she had gone from being a prisoner to a hostage. Would Simon de Montfort have her killed if Edward refused to give himself up? Eleanor doubted he would. It would be foolish to risk his reputation and would certainly cost him more followers. But the threat was still there.

In the days that followed, gossip trickled in. Perhaps the guards were being bribed, or perhaps they were concerned about their future should Prince Edward succeed.

Eleanor learned that the marcher lords had joined Prince Edward and bolstered his forces with reinforcements from Scotland. In a stroke of luck, the Earl of Gloucester defected to Edward's side.

The news was good. As far as she knew, Simon de Montfort was scrambling to raise an army to try and destroy Edward before he rallied even more people to his cause.

The days ticked by, and Eleanor watched from the window of her apartment for any sign of what was going on in the world outside.

As it happened, she wasn't at her window to see Edward ride into the courtyard, and was caught completely off guard when he strode into her apartments looking triumphant.

"Edward," she called out, jumping to her feet. "My God. You are here!"

Ignoring all decorum she ran into his arms, and he embraced her with a laugh that shook his whole body.

"We are restored, my love."

"And you are alive," she said. "Nothing else matters."

He grinned down at her. "That is not entirely true. You wouldn't wish to be married to a peasant farmer."

She scoffed. "It is you I love. If you were a farmer, I would go out into the fields and reap the wheat at your side. Perhaps we'd have a few pigs to fatten for our supper too."

"Enough of this talk. I will one day be king and you my queen," he said, kissing her.

"And Simon?"

A strange look passed over Edward's face. "He is dead."

"Ah."

"His army has scattered, but there are still pockets of rebellion in our kingdom that we will have to root out."

"Where is your father?"

"He's with the main army. But I left them to hurry back to you. I needed to make sure you were safe. My father will make his way back to Westminster and you will have to help tend to him, for I fear he has suffered at Simon's hands."

"You make it sound as though you are about to leave again," Eleanor said, frowning. Her grip on his arms tightened as though she could hold him here in this room forever.

"I will have to, but not tonight. Tonight I came to be with you and our child. We are restored to our lands and titles. Slowly, we will rebuild our wealth and strengthen this kingdom again."

"Won't your father have anything to say about that?" she asked, her tone teasing.

He pulled her towards the bed, a mischievous grin on his face. "*I* am the victor of Evesham. Not my father."

"He will have you crowned King?" she gasped.

"No. But I might as well be. When you see my father you will understand. He is a defeated, tired man, but I don't wish to step into his shoes just yet."

She wondered why, but was too distracted by his heated kisses to ask him more.

After Edward bid her farewell the following day, she took over the running of the palace, preparing it for the return of the King. All of Simon's emblems were destroyed and Eleanor moved to better accommodations.

The Londoners in the city outside were in an uncertain mood, and knowing how unpopular King Henry and Queen Alienor were among them, Eleanor sent out free wine and ale from the storerooms for the Mayor to distribute to all the guilds. She announced a celebration to mark the defeat of Simon de Montfort and sat in the Queen's seat in the great hall that night.

Elsewhere, her husband was leading the royal army, pursuing his enemies to the very end.

Free as she was, Eleanor was still stuck waiting for news, but the shadow that had hung over her was lifted. She felt lighthearted as she went about her day.

King Henry returned with all pomp and ceremony to the capital, as he awaited Queen Alienor's return from France. Indeed, he had become feeble since the last time she'd seen him. He often took to his bed and Eleanor tried to coax him to walk with her as often as she could.

"We are both doomed to wait for our spouses," she said to him one day as they sat in the herb garden.

He chuckled. "I suppose there are worse fates."

"Has Queen Alienor written to you? I have received news that the English navy is patrolling the seas waiting to escort her ship home."

King Henry looked wistfully up at the sky. "She'll come home and then there will be peace at last."

Eleanor smiled. "Peace is within our grasp, but I don't know if it will last. There is always another war to fight, and your son has great ambitions."

The King laughed, and the booming sound reminded Eleanor of Edward. Her heart yearned for her absent husband all over again. "His desires will take him far from you," said the King. "You should not encourage him."

Eleanor shook her head. "No. Long ago I swore that I would be at his side no matter where he went. The next time he goes on campaign, I shall go with him."

"Yet he didn't he take you this time?"

Eleanor looked sheepishly down at her lap. "I have told no one yet, but I am with child again. I hope this one will be a son to cement Edward's victory at Evesham. We will call him Henry, after you."

King Henry withdrew from her then, his face twisting with horror. "Evesham? No — that wasn't a victory."

"What do you mean?" she said with a breathy laugh, thinking he was making a jest.

"No. I was there. It was a massacre. Edward's army outnumbered Simon's and had the high ground. Still Simon sent his men up that hill," King Henry said, shaking his head sorrowfully. "There was so much death. So much destruction. Even when they surrendered the killing went on. No. I wouldn't call it a victory."

Eleanor's good humor melted away at his words. Her mouth was dry and she wanted to refute his words, but how could she? The thought of Edward being so brutal as to slaughter defeated men sent a chill to the very core of her being.

Simon de Montfort deserved no pity for inciting rebellion and discord in the country, but did the men who were honor bound to follow their lord deserve such brutality?

"There will be much to atone for. But do not fret. Tell me, when do you think the baby will be born? We will have to cast its horoscope. I have an amazing astrologer in my employ." He reached over and patted her cold hands.

Edward returned at the head of the royal army. They had chased Simon de Montfort's son all the way to Winchelsea and cornered him in the city there.

After a long siege, the town had fallen and the last leader of the de Montfort faction lay dead.

Eleanor welcomed her husband back with open arms but couldn't help noticing a hardness in his features that had never been there before.

"Welcome home, Prince Edward," she said formally, and curtseyed formally.

He lifted her up and led her to his father, who was waiting on his throne.

Edward unsheathed his sword and laid it at his father's feet before kneeling for his blessing.

"Rise, my son," King Henry said. "Welcome home."

The two men embraced to the cheering of the court.

The Earl of Gloucester came next to prostrate himself before the King. He begged for forgiveness and swore fealty to the Crown. Eleanor's attention never wavered from Edward, and she longed to speak with him alone.

As they sat to dine, she squeezed his hand. "My Lord, are you well?"

"As can be," he said, his tone monotonous. Seeing her concern he forced a smile. "I am just tired and there is so much to do before I can feel secure."

Eleanor glanced around. All the nobles of England seemed to be here. Who was there left to fight?

———————

The following morning she woke to find the bed beside her empty.

Slipping into a gown, she went in search of her husband and found him sitting beneath an apple tree, staring up at the sky.

Wrapping the mantle tightly around herself she approached tentatively. "Husband, have you abandoned me so soon after your return?"

He smiled up at her. "I couldn't sleep."

Eleanor sat down beside him. Despite her wool mantle she shivered, and he wrapped his own cloak around her too.

"You ought to go back inside," he whispered.

"Only if you tell me what ails you."

He couldn't meet her eyes and she felt anxiety coursing through her.

"I have read that there is no honor in battle," she said, "only death. It is common for rage to overcome reason."

"You speak of Evesham," Edward guessed.

She nodded. "You've been different since your return. It's as if there's a fog between us and I cannot find you. Edward, you did what you had to. You were victorious. You will confess to your sins and be absolved of them. Then you must focus on the future."

His eyes flicked back to the sky above. "No priest can absolve me of the sin I carry. But you are right. That is the way of the world. If I had not defeated Simon, then he would've killed me and you would not have been safe. Even if I could go back, I wouldn't do anything different. But I will have to live with the memories my whole life."

"Your men love and respect you. Everyone praises your cunning and strength. One day soon you will be a great king."

Again Edward nodded. "And what does it say about me that I am willing to pay the price to make that dream come true?"

Eleanor frowned. "You can choose a different path. You once asked if I would have liked to be married to you if you were a farmer, and in jest I said yes. But I wasn't joking. I would follow you to the ends of the world if I had to. No matter what you chose. I will stand by your side."

He tilted her chin up to him and placed a kiss on her lips. "I don't deserve you."

"Yes, you do."

The following day, King Henry left to await Queen Alienor's arrival from France. Eleanor spent the time preparing for their return. They would arrive in a grand procession, and she planned for them to be greeted along the way by well-wishers, musicians and acrobats.

A feast grander than the one they had at Christmas would be prepared with every delicacy imaginable. Edward encouraged her and she dove into her work, happy for the distraction.

When King Henry and Queen Alienor returned, the people cheered, but they reserved their love for Edward, who rode in full armor behind them.

He had become a hero.

Stories of his escape from Hereford had become legend, and his victory over Simon de Montfort had cemented his popularity.

That night the celebrations in the city were loud enough to be heard in the palace. Whether or not the Londoners supported the King and Queen, they were certainly eager to celebrate the warrior Prince who had delivered them from years of uncertainty. Edward was already hailed as a peace bringer and uniter of the realm.

As they listened to the singing in the streets below, Eleanor leaned against him. Tonight, as he was celebrated by the court, he had been truly happy for the first time in days. He had even danced with her and laughed with wild abandon as though they were back in Gascony.

"You have achieved everything we ever hoped for," said Eleanor. "Those people out there, they look to you as their de facto king. We have secured our lands and have a growing brood of children. What shall you do next? Are we to retire to some country manor?"

He pushed back her hair so he could study her closely. "No, I have been preparing myself for what is to come. My path has been laid out for me and I cannot veer off course now. I will fulfill my promise and go on crusade. It will happen soon; the French are preparing already."

She met his gaze, waiting for him to speak of Evesham,

but as always he remained resolutely silent. "And I will be at your side when you do."

"Eleanor, I will need someone here to ensure—"

She fixed him with a look that silenced him. "I, too, made a promise, and I intend to keep it."

"I fought to ensure your safety and regain control over the realm. Now you are telling me you'd venture out into new dangers?"

"Certainly." Eleanor arched a delicate brow, taking hold of his hand. "Our battle is never over."

EPILOGUE

1272, THE HOLY LAND

The air was heavy with the scent of sandalwood mingled with the sweat of men as they argued in the council chamber. Normally, this would be a formal affair attended by the noble commanders and rulers of the region, but after the latest disaster on the battlefield, there was no need for privacy.

This suited Eleanor, who sat off to the side on an inconspicuous stool, her eyes demurely downcast as she listened to the men shout at each other.

"How did this happen?"

"Why were the men not kept in check?"

"Who was in command?"

The questions came so quickly it was unclear who was speaking. Did it matter? Eleanor didn't think so. Just like the answers to these pertinent questions would not bring back the men who died trying to storm Qaqun. They were now dead and the hopes of retaking Jerusalem lost with them. At least for now, as in time, she was sure, there would always be more men, eager to try their luck at reconquering the Holy Land.

She smoothed a hand over her gown. The soft linen fabric was made in these lands and completely foreign to her. From the loose fit of the dress to the brilliant shade of red, nothing was like what she was used to. Compared to the heavy wool gowns she had arrived with from England, these felt weightless. Upon arriving in Acre, she quickly discovered how impractical her old gowns were. Stubbornly, she kept wearing her damask and wool gowns until the heat of summer came. Then she had to relent and accept defeat.

"We would've succeeded if reinforcements had not come. Which is why I had instructed Lord Geoffrey to bring his men to block off the eastern passage," Prince Edward said. His voice was like a low growl.

Eleanor allowed her gaze to slide over to her husband. His back was turned to her so he did not see the slight pursing of her lips.

It had been his decision to lead out his men in this attempt to capture the city. There had been sickness and drought. Spies had reported that a contingent of men had ridden out to join the army of Berber. There would never be a better time to launch an attack. This had felt like their best chance to take the city.

And so they tried.

But they didn't account for the heat of the day or how long it would take the breakdown the gates while their men were pelted by arrows and stones.

Once they had broken through, there was still more fighting.

If Eleanor closed her eyes, she thought she could imagine the winding streets of that smaller town as the men made their way through. They would've been unfamiliar with the terrain and the defenders fought fiercely, for they had women and children to defend.

They were evenly matched until a fresh contingent of soldiers arrived to bolster the numbers of the enemy.

Edward should've called for a retreat sooner, but the heat of the day and the exhilaration of battle blew away all rational thought. He had scented victory in the air and could not see defeat coming for him.

It would help if the armies gathered here could see the wisdom of trusting one another. But these great commanders all dreamed of attaining glory and could be self-serving. Eleanor kept these realizations to herself, for she didn't have a solution.

Edward had fallen into a foul temper, ever since illness had decimated their forces in Sicily. He was deaf to any advice or criticism. So Eleanor stopped wasting her breath.

"Prince Edward, while valiant, we told you it was too soon. The region is defended by more than just men. The terrain is rough and the heat makes it hard for our men to fight."

"It was the best chance we had, and we failed," Edward said. His palm landed on the table with a heavy thud. It might have been seen as a disrespectful act by King Hugh of Cyprus if all the men at the council had thought this was simply the uncouth manners of the English.

They talked at length about the failed campaign, tallying up their losses and what they had learned. Servants came in to replace the oil lamps and bring in trays of dates and nuts for the men to eat.

Only when the moon was high overhead did the meeting draw to a close. Exhaustion was evident on the face of every man.

Eleanor stood and fell into step beside Edward. He held her hand as they made their way through the palace. They stepped to the side as a passing woman ran past, carrying a crying infant. Eleanor felt a pang of concern. Her mind turned from matters of war to her own children back in England. A wave of sadness swept over her and she found she had stopped walking. Edward looked questioningly at her, but she shook her head and gave him a little smile. She did not want to talk about it.

They pressed on. Only when they were behind the closed doors of their private apartments did he turn to her.

"And what is your opinion, my love? Have I failed once again?"

She looked up into his eyes. A harshness tempered the bright eyes she usually found so striking. It had been there, marring his features, ever since he had returned from the Battle of Lewes. Not even the birth of their son six years ago had made it vanish.

Even though it was a necessity and source of pride that her husband was such a valiant warrior, Eleanor still hated what war did to him.

"It was a defeat but I believe you acted with the best of intentions. No one could've predicted the outcome. Given the knowledge we had, you did the best you could. Your strategy was not to blame."

"Only the execution of it," he said, his tone full of

morose as he pulled away from her and found his way to a nearby table where a jug of wine awaited him.

"The simple truth is you need more men," she said, smiling to herself at this old complaint. Would she be repeating this sentiment for the rest of her life as she had in Gascony?

"If only we could come together under one commander," Edward said, as he poured wine into two cups and handed her one of them.

"And who would you appoint?" She asked, taking a delicate sip. Then grinned at his expression. "I do believe it should be you but I am sure the rest feel the same about themselves."

"It's a hopeless business. When we set out on Crusade, I had not imagined this."

"I don't think you are the first or the last to express such sentiments. We can return to England. Your father would be grateful to you if you did."

Edward shook his head. "We would inevitably quarrel. My mother has never forgotten who it was that saved the crown and while she might be grateful, she still wants to assert herself as ruler supreme."

"Then perhaps we can go to Gascony."

He shrugged. Clearly, his heart was not in it. His ambitions had grown larger than ruling one measly province.

"While we figure out what to do, let us rest. We will be useless to everyone if we cannot think straight." She led him gently over to their bed.

The servants had been dismissed, so it fell to her to help him undress.

Before he drifted off to sleep, he tucked an arm around her and buried his head in the crook of her neck.

Eleanor found that sleep evaded her and she stared up at the canopy above them. For all his faults, she loved this man beside her with a fierceness that stunned her at times. Even when she knew he was wrong, she trusted he would learn and make up for his mistakes. She'd seen him be kind, seen him be cruel, but all the while, his loyalty to her remained constant. Now she was determined they had to return home. He had done all he could in the Holy Land. The longer they stayed, the more likely it was that he would succumb to some strange ailment or his anger and it would be disastrous for them all.

As she closed her eyes she imagined their children left in the care of their grandparents back in England. John would be six years old this year and Henry, just shy of five. Then there was their youngest, a daughter named Eleanor, who was just barely a year old when they had first departed. She'd be three now. Did she remember her mother at all?

Were they healthy? Were they safe?

Eleanor rolled on her side, trying to shut out these thoughts that nagged at her. Her children were both a source of pride and great sadness for her. She'd already buried two daughters and couldn't stomach the thought that she might lose the others. When her thoughts turned to their lands in England and Gascony, she longed to return. Here in Acre, Eleanor felt like she'd been cast adrift without a purpose. If only she could be more resilient.

Edward murmured into her ear. "What ails you, my love?"

"Can I not have a moment alone?" She whispered back, half laughing, half crying.

"It is hard to sleep when your wife cries at your side."

"I made no sound."

"We are of one mind." He wiped her cheek with his thumb. "Though, to be honest, I felt the rhythm of your breath change."

She couldn't see in the dark but she could feel him smiling against the skin of her neck.

"Be at peace, my love. All is well in our realm and with our children." Edward held her tight against him and in the warmth of his embrace all her concerns were vanquished.

With nothing to do, Eleanor kept herself busy in the following days. She visited the markets with a maid and armed guard, walked along the path overlooking the Mediterranean Sea and enjoyed stargazing in the evening.

The weeks slipped by as Edward rode out on patrol and trained with his men. Finally, when his duties were done, he returned to their apartments and drew her into his plans.

In public, he might not openly ask for her opinions, but here in private he enjoyed debating the various battle plans he had drawn up for a future attack on Qaqun.

"I know my enemy better now," he said, musing over the crudely drawn maps. "If we can get through the southern gate or better yet draw them out from behind the walls then our cavalry could charge."

Eleanor grimaced at the thought of so much destruction. She'd seen the realities of war often enough that she should've become numb to it. Instead, she found eager for the day when her husband could put down his sword and focus on other matters.

"King Hugh may not allow another excursion. Acre is poorly defended as it is. Can we afford to lose more men?"

Edward frowned at her. "I'll convince him."

She let out a breath. Would he listen if she told him the mood in the city was uneasy? Merchants were skittish as colts, ready to bolt at the first sign of danger. It was growing apparent to all that matters were grave as the Sultan Baybars gained more power in the region, while the crusaders bled allies and resources with no sign of reprieve.

In May, despite Edward's fervent hopes for war, King Hugh signed a peace treaty with the Sultan. In exchange for the return of hostages and gold, there would be a truce lasting ten years.

Edward had gone red with fury upon hearing the announcement.

"I will not stand for it! I will not sign. My men and I will do as we please."

Then he stormed out of the council chamber, leaving Eleanor feeling, for the first time, ashamed of her husband. The King's expression was stony as he turned to the rest of the men and apologized to the ambassador from the Sultan.

Eleanor turned on her heel and went in search of Edward.

She found him sitting beneath an olive tree, throwing

stones against a far wall. This was hardly the picture of a fierce warrior.

"My love, you are angry. But perhaps this is a sign that we are to return home."

"No. Baybars will not honor the terms of the peace and within the year, he will be attacking us again."

Eleanor saw the truth of this. "You are right. Peace treaties rarely hold but it will buy us time to resupply. The fight has gone out of the men here. They need to rest. They need to have something to hope for."

Edward grunted but was resolute to keep sulking in the courtyard, so Eleanor retreated inside. King Hugh came upon her just as she was headed to the library.

"Princess, I meant to speak with you and I hope now is as good a time as any?"

She curtseyed and said, "Certainly, Your Grace. How may I be of service?"

"Your husband is a passionate man. I admire his — ambitions, but he cannot gainsay me in front of my lords and the ambassadors like that again." There was an edge of anger to his tone, tempered by long years of experience.

"I know it creates discord among the men to see their commanders at odds with one another," Eleanor said, eyes meeting his. "I will speak to him. It is just as likely that he knows he made a mistake and regrets losing his temper. When he set his mind to join this crusade, he did it with a single-minded purpose of retaking Jerusalem. It is disappointing to find that reality must constrain his dreams."

"I have heard that you are wise and am happy to find that it is so," the King said, inclining his head in a little bow.

"If you should ever require my assistance, I will provide it. Even if it is ships and funds to return home."

"That is most kind," Eleanor said, and with another curtsey, watched him go.

In the coming days, even though Edward no longer contradicted the King publicly, it was becoming evident that they were no longer welcome in Acre but merely tolerated.

"Have you thought of returning home?" Eleanor said, as they watched a merchant ship unloading its wares.

"Not yet. This treaty might still fall apart," Edward said.

"As long as it is not because of your interference." She rested her head against his shoulder. "You've stirred up enough trouble for the King."

"I am a Prince, that is what I do. But I swear to you I have not been plotting."

May gave way to June and on the day of the Feast of Corpus Christi, Acre observed the holy day with a large procession through the streets and a solemn feast at the palace. The day had been long and exhausting but Eleanor found sleep was evading her and so sat at her writing desk reading the missives they received from England by oil lamp. Shadows danced around the room as her maid waiting nearby fought back a yawn.

"You may retire if —" Eleanor's words were cut off by the doors to her rooms being thrown open. Caught by surprise, she leaped to her feet, ready to scream. It was merely Edgar, her husband's page, and she immediately relaxed, ready to castigate him for intruding upon her like this.

"My lady! Come quick," he said.

All at once Eleanor felt her throat clench. "What has happened?" she asked.

"Prince Edward was attacked. He killed the man, but he's been wounded. He asked for you."

Eleanor's knees felt weak. "Take me to him."

Out in the hall there was such a commotion, Eleanor wasn't sure how she had not heard it before. Edgar led her through the gathered people and brought her to a room adjoining Edward's.

He was thrashing about on a makeshift bed, his eyes closed, as two doctors busied themselves tending to a wound on his arm. In the room, the King and his marshal stood, heads bowed in deep discussion.

Eleanor pushed past them, forgoing any decorum, as she dropped to her knees at his side. "My love, what has happened to you?"

At the sound of her voice, Edward stilled before the thrashing began again.

"He's been poisoned, My Lady," one doctor said. "We are trying to clean the wound, but there isn't much we can do besides pray."

In the fear of grip, Eleanor felt at a loss for words. "An antidote? Surely you must have one?"

"We will try."

From the way the doctor spoke, he did not sound certain and Eleanor felt the edges of her vision fade. She gritted her teeth refusing to succumb to such weakness. Edward needed her.

"The wound was not deep. There is hope, Princess."

Eleanor looked up to see the King speaking to her.

"We must trust these good men to do their work."

"I will stay by his side," she said, daring him to contradict her.

"As you wish," he said.

"How did this happen? Who is responsible?" Eleanor asked, in a moment of clarity, as she gripped Edward's uninjured hand.

"An assassin sent, no doubt, by the Sultan. I do not know how he got through our defenses. But he is dead and he cannot be questioned on the details. I worry about all our safety."

Eleanor frowned, but turned her attention back to her husband.

For three days, Edward waged a war with the poison coursing through his veins. Only on the fourth day did the fever and convulsions break. He was weak but coherent and Eleanor found she could at last let herself weep.

"Stop it, my love," Edward said. He was propped up in bed by pillows, as he was too tired to stand. She did not stop until he reached over to tilt her face up to his. "I have survived and will recover. You need not cry now."

"I cry because I am so relieved. Edward, I feared the worst. I need you. Your children need you. Please —" She stopped, unsure what she wanted to ask, but he seemed to guess.

"While I slept I dreamed of England," Edward said, with a forlorn expression. "I long to see my home again. In my folly, I have endangered myself and you. It is time we return home."

Eleanor let out a gasp of surprise. "Truly?"

"I have done all I can here." Then, with a rueful grin added, "and I can tell when I am not wanted."

With a laugh, Eleanor threw her arms around Edward's neck and embraced him. He nearly toppled against her and she drew back, apologizing.

"If I had listened to my wife's wise advice, I would not be in such a predicament," he teased, though she could see how rattled he was by his brush with death.

"It is always a battle trying to make you listen," she said, as she slid onto the bed beside him.

"A battle I hope you will always keep fighting."

She craned her head up to peer into his eyes. "For as long as I draw breath, I promise."

AUTHOR'S NOTE

Eleanor of Castile would become Queen of England in 1272, after King Henry's death, alongside her husband King Edward I. At the time of her father-in-law's death the pair returning from Acre and it took some months before they returned to England.

Edward would become a renowned warrior and fierce ruler with a hot temper. As King, Edward would go on to conquer Wales and planned to do the same in Scotland. He could be brutal in his dealings with his enemies. Though his reign was regarded as being successful, his cruelty cast a shadow on his successes. How Eleanor felt about his actions is unknown but they remained devoted to each other.

Edward and Eleanor's son Edward (born in 1284) was the first English prince to carry the title "Prince of Wales". From then on, the heir to the English crown was usually bestowed with this title.

Tragically, of the sixteen children Eleanor bore Edward, few survived to adulthood and even fewer outlived her.

After the death of her mother, she became Countess of

Ponthieu, meaning the province also came under English control. While she was alive, Eleanor accompanied her husband on all his campaigns. Their unwillingness to be apart is further evidence that they loved and valued each other dearly.

Eleanor died in 1290. Sources are unclear as to why, but they suspect childbirth was the primary cause. Throughout her life and reign she patronized the arts and collected an impressive library for the time. While many of her contemporaries disapproved of how she acquired lands, they viewed her in a more positive light compared to Queen Alienor. Like Alienor, Eleanor promoted her relatives, but she was careful when she did so and most of the marriages she arranged were of female relatives to English noblemen, and thus were less upsetting to the general public.

Edward was greatly distressed by Eleanor's death. To commemorate her memory he commissioned the Eleanor Crosses. These impressive stone structures are a mark of Edward's power and love for her. Three survive to this day.

Printed in Great Britain
by Amazon

46334470R00138